I0550563

SAM CRESCENT

EVERNIGHT PUBLISHING ®

www.evernightpublishing.com

Copyright© 2020

Sam Crescent

Editor: Karyn White

Cover Artist: Jay Aheer

ISBN: 978-0-3695-0268-1

ALL RIGHTS RESERVED

WARNING: The unauthorized reproduction or distribution of this copyrighted work is illegal. No part of this book may be used or reproduced electronically or in print without written permission, except in the case of brief quotations embodied in reviews.

This is a work of fiction. All names, characters, and places are fictitious. Any resemblance to actual events, locales, organizations, or persons, living or dead, is entirely coincidental.

SAM CRESCENT

Curvy Women Wanted, 13

Sam Crescent

Copyright © 2019

Chapter One

Theo West waited for the perfect moment to approach Ruby James. His friends were all gathered around, talking about the game last Friday. A couple of cheerleaders were hanging off their arms as they spoke. It was just like every other day. Guys and girls passed them in the school halls, and each person was desperate to catch someone else's eye. Theo didn't have time for that bullshit right now. He was focused on only one girl. He'd not seen her yet and knew she wasn't going to the cafeteria first, as he'd been watching her for six months.

She always came to her locker to put away her books.

For six months she hadn't done anything different, and he doubted today the beautiful blonde would even consider doing anything like it. His locker was nowhere near hers, but he had the perfect excuse for watching her. He was standing with his football buddies.

His friends were starting to move on, slamming locker doors closed, and she still hadn't made an appearance, which really pissed him off.

"Hey, Theo, what are you doing tonight?" Rachel asked. She was one of the best cheerleaders on the squad and had been trying to get with him for some time. He had no interest in putting his dick anywhere near her. She was often the main discussion in the shower room where most of the guys talked about how she liked to fuck. He didn't want any part of that. Not that he had a problem with sex. Not at all. He loved sex. What he didn't want was Rachel.

The girl that had been starring in his fantasies of late just so happened to round the corner before he and his guys left for the cafeteria. Mike, his best friend, who also happened to know whom he wanted, smirked at him.

"See you soon." Mike shook his hand and took off, leaving him alone with Ruby.

Her face was red, and she looked really frustrated as she got to the locker. He watched as she twisted the dial back and forth, before waiting for the door to open.

The school was old, and so were their lockers. She had to bang the door three times for it to open. Most of them had to do the same.

"Hey, Ruby," he said.

"Theo, what's up?" she asked.

He waited as she opened up her bag, putting three books inside before grabbing out three more.

"Why does there have to be something up?" He folded his arms across his chest and leaned against the locker. She closed her door, and her face was no longer hidden to him. She pulled her bag on, watching him.

"Were you waiting for me?"

"No." That was a total lie. Of course he was.

She smiled. "Then what's up? It's not like you to stand around waiting for me." She tilted her head to the side. Her face had lost the red color.

Her pale skin looked so soft, he wanted to reach out and stroke it. He couldn't pinpoint the exact moment in his life when he realized that he wanted her, only that it had become an obsession of his.

"I've been thinking we should go out some time."

She started to chuckle. "Okay, good joke." She made to move past, going in the opposite direction of the cafeteria.

He didn't expect that kind of reaction from her. "It's not a joke." He grabbed her arm, stopping her from leaving. This wasn't going how he intended at all.

"Theo, what's going on? I'm kind of confused at the moment." She stared at her arm where he held her, and he had to force himself to let her go, even though he didn't want to.

"I want to take you on a date."

"Theo, you do know I'm Ruby, right? I'm not on the cheerleading squad or, like, associated in any way with football, or sports in general." She licked her lips, and he wanted to kiss her.

"I know. Just because you're not part of the team doesn't mean we can't hang out."

"We've never hung out. Like, ever."

He was used to chicks being all over him. He was one of the most popular guys in school. With just the snap of his fingers he could have any girl, and yet the one he wanted looked at him like a crazy person.

"Let's change that."

She shook her head. "I don't think so." She pulled away, and he couldn't think of a single thing to say to make her stop.

That was not what he wanted.

Running fingers through his hair, he watched her ass sway. He stared until her curvy body was no longer in sight before heading toward the cafeteria where Mike had already gotten him a tray of food.

"How did it go?"

"Bad," he said.

"Really? Wow, that does surprise me," Mike said.

Theo took a bite of his burger and looked toward his friend. "Why does that surprise you?"

"I bet you a hundred bucks you approach every single chick in this room, they'd jump at the chance to go out with you. Ruby isn't popular. She doesn't have guys hanging off her every word, but you, my friend, are like a sex magnet. I don't get it. Clearly she's a lesbo."

"She didn't believe my offer for a date was genuine." He took another bite.

"You're not going to give up, are you?"

"Hell, no."

Mike laughed. "So, what's the game? You want to fuck this chick or something?"

"You know it's not about that."

"You got to be prepared to deal with the consequences. A guy like you, messing with a chick like her, it's going to bite you in the ass."

Theo felt the anger simmer beneath the surface. "A girl like what?" he asked.

"You know, fat."

The blood pounded in Theo's temples. It pissed him off to think of anyone calling Ruby fat. She was a beautiful, sexy woman. One he wanted more than anything.

****

"I've just had the weirdest experience of all high school," Ruby said, entering the kitchen back at home.

It was just her and her mother and had been for

nearly eight years now, when her father up and left saying he couldn't handle this life anymore. Last they had heard he was pursuing some kind of Wall Street job. He sent money every single month to deal with the rent and expenses. As far as Ruby could tell, her mother was no longer heartbroken over it, but she also never dated either.

"You were forced to eat chocolate as the best kind of adult experience of your life?" Callie asked.

"I wish." She dropped her bag on the floor and jumped up on the opposite side of where her mother was working. She worked long hours at the local vet's and was often on call to help out. Ruby wondered if the main veterinarian, Steven, had a bit of a crush on her mother. He was ten years older, and always flirting. Her mother never noticed of course.

Callie was rolling out dough, cutting large circles and placing some pulled pork mixture on to one half of the dough, sealing it up, crimping the edges, and placing them onto baking sheets.

Glancing over at the calendar, Ruby saw it was the day her mother always filled the freezer. This helped them throughout the month in case something ever came up and they didn't like ordering takeout. Her mother was an amazing cook. Rolling up her sleeves, Ruby jumped off the counter and washed her hands.

"If it has nothing to do with chocolate, which it totally should, let's see … you got asked out?"

Ruby dried her hands and nodded. "Yep. I got asked out."

"Oh, that is so wonderful." Callie turned to her with a huge smile.

"Yeah, the most popular boy in school asked me out."

"And?"

"And, it's got to be some kind of trick, right?"

"Why does it have to be some kind of trick?"

"Seriously, Mom, when have I ever mentioned Theo West, or even had him turn up on my doorstep?" She shrugged.

"Okay, never."

"It has to be some kind of trick. There's no other explanation for it."

"I really don't like this negativity from you. It's the one trait you get from your father, and it's really not healthy."

She rolled her eyes. "I'm being serious. Why would a guy like Theo want to be with a girl like me? For one, I hate sports. I've never, ever gone to a game."

"Then go to a game."

"I can't go to a game," she said.

"You know, sweetie, I hate to say this to you, but you're the one being really difficult here."

"I'm the one being difficult?"

"Yes. You really shouldn't worry your head so much." She chuckled. Her mother dusted off her hands and turned to face her. "First of all, you're a beautiful woman. I know you don't see it, but you really are. You turn heads when we go shopping together. You catch men's eyes. Second, you're smart. So intelligent, apart from when you're being stubborn, and then you lose all of that intelligence down the toilet."

"Mom."

"Third, you're a nice person. You're not mean to anyone, and for me, you have been the perfect daughter. One I'm so proud of. I can see why every single man would love to be with you. You've just got to learn to see it yourself." Her mother cupped her face and pressed a kiss to her forehead.

"What if it's a joke?" Ruby said.

"Then we'll figure it out. You know my stance on trusting you."

"How can you be so trusting after what Dad did?"

Callie sighed. "Your father was never the settling down type. You know this. We had you by accident."

She knew her parents were due to go off to college when her mother got pregnant. Her father went to college, and, so his parents would help support them, her mother stayed at home. If Callie hadn't gotten pregnant, Ruby had no doubt she'd be a veterinarian right now rather than Steven.

"He was the popular guy in school, and our relationship was doomed to fail from the start."

"Did you ever consider it doomed?" Ruby asked.

"No, I don't consider it a failure now. We've moved on. We have different ideas of what we want out of life." Her mother kissed her head. "Stop being so negative before I've got to call your father and berate him for being an ass and rubbing off on you."

Ruby chuckled.

"You want to finish helping me with these pies?"

"Love to."

They got to work, and Ruby cut out each pie shape as her mother filled and shaped them.

"So, tell me, is this guy cute?"

She thought about Theo. "He's … not the boy next door. His persona is very boy next door, but he has short black hair. Blue eyes. He works out a lot. He looks more like the teacher than the student." She heard her mother chuckle. "What?"

"For a girl that's not interested, you sure know how to describe him."

"He's not hot or anything. I don't know. I've never really noticed him."

"Wait a moment, Theo West?"

"Yes."

"He's got a Labrador that got into his stash of chocolate just last week. He came in so concerned. We had to help the dog bring the chocolate back up, and it still was in the wrappers. He seemed like a nice boy. Handsome too."

"Mom?"

"What, I can't be encouraging to my very negative daughter?"

"You should be advising me against doing anything. You do know guys in this generation demand sex, right?"

"Honey, guys in every single generation demand sex. They just hid it better in the past is all. Besides, you know your body, and your mind. Do you need me to repeat no means no, and to leave and to not be forced to do something?"

"No."

"What about the safe sex?"

"No."

"Good. I won't push you into dating, but try not to be so cynical so young. It'll give you wrinkles."

Chapter Two

The following day, Theo wasn't going to allow one failed attempt to woo this girl to put him off. If she was completely dead set against dating him, then he'd step back, but for now, he had a feeling she was … scared. He'd never had a chick turn him down before and he wasn't looking forward to the experience again any time soon, but he liked Ruby.

She wasn't like any of the other girls he'd ever met.

Running finger through his hair, he spotted her, and he saw when she did him. She walked up toward him, looking hesitant. The one plus for him, she didn't turn on her heel and run in the opposite direction.

Squaring his shoulders, he waited.

"Hey, Theo," she said, approaching her locker.

He noticed several guys and girls watching them. He wasn't interested in any of them, just the girl in front of him now.

Today her long blonde hair had a slight curl to it as it fell down her back and over her chest. It always looked so silken even after gym. She wore no makeup. He'd never known her to wear any in all the years he'd been watching her.

"What's up?" she asked.

"I know you said no yesterday, but I want to take you on a date."

She didn't immediately shut him down. He considered that a plus.

"There's a pizza place that just opened up."

"It's Fabio's place. I've heard of it," she said.

"Would you like to go out with me for pizza?" he asked.

His hands were shaking, so he shoved them into

his back pocket. This wasn't going how he hoped.

Girls usually screamed, or at least they did in the past.

"Can you answer me something first?"

"Sure."

"Why?"

"I like pizza. I figured everyone liked pizza."

She laughed. "It's not about the pizza. I was wondering why you're asking *me*? We don't really talk and we've never hung out, and yet, you're asking me for pizza. See the problem I'm having here?"

"True. It's not a joke. I like you, and in all honesty, I've been wanting to ask you out for some time but never got around to it."

"Never got around to it?"

"No. Between football, college, and stuff—"

"You're going to college?"

"That's the plan."

"Cool. I didn't know you were set on going to college."

"I've got a few options open to me. I keep my head down, get decent grades, and I do try. I didn't think I'd get too far without it. It's a lot of hard work, which I'm always willing to do. I want to be more than a high school jock."

He saw he'd surprised her, which he'd take. He'd take anything so long as it would get her on a date with him.

"Okay, we'll go for pizza."

"This Friday, after the game?"

"Yeah, this Friday."

"Do you need me to talk to your mom or something?" His father had told him about Ruby's parents breaking up so he didn't have to worry about her dad anytime soon.

"Nah, it's fine. She'll be fine with it. See you this Friday after the game."

"Are you coming to the game?"

"Nope. I'll get my mom to drive me, and I'll meet you."

They arranged a place to meet, and by the time they finished, the bell for first classes sounded.

Theo wanted to kiss her, but he also didn't want to spook her. Walking her to class, he ran toward his own, and got there just in time before the door closed.

He found Mike in the back, and took a seat next to him.

"You got her to say yes?"

"I've got her phone number." He held it up in victory. Now, all he needed to do was to convince Ruby that he was a sure deal.

There was no joke attached to him wanting to date her, not even a small one. Mike had thought there was when he first mentioned his feelings for Ruby, but his best friend soon realized he meant business and had stopped trying to tease him over it. While the English teacher started to go on about some poem, he pulled out his cell phone and typed in her number, saving it.

Theo: **Got your number saved, Theo. X**

He thought about adding an emoji and quickly decided against it. A X was serious, he liked to think.

Stop being a pussy when it comes to this girl.

Ruby: **You should be listening to your teacher.**

Theo: **I like to live dangerously.**

Ruby: **I like to graduate.**

Theo: **Be a good girl and study.**

He didn't get a response back, but he was already feeling positive from her responses. Today was going to be one hell of a good day.

****

Ruby had a nightmare week after accepting Theo's date. Her phone was confiscated by the teacher as she was caught putting it in her bag. The math teacher then decided to read out all the messages from Theo, which only served to make her embarrassed, and for all the popular girls to point out that she wasn't the real kind of girl that he liked to date.

As if she didn't already know that!

She did get her cell phone back at the end of the day but with a strict warning to not get it out during class again. Her mother laughed at the entire incident and even made a comment about there not being cell phones when she was in high school. It was always folded-up notes they passed

"I don't think you should drop me off," Ruby said.

"You've got your cell phone, and if you're not happy with how your date is going, call me. You know I'll answer no matter what."

"I don't like this, Mom."

"You're going to have fun tonight."

"That sounded like an order."

"It was." Her mother chuckled.

Releasing the seatbelt, Ruby stared out into the night, wishing for something to come up. A random phone call, anything that would stop her from getting out of the car. Nothing came. Opening the door, she said a final goodbye to her mother, who gave her a thumbs-up. She stood in the parking lot just as the last car drove away.

Rubbing her hands together to ward off the chill, she spun toward the main high school building. Football meant a great deal to a lot of people in town. She'd never shared the same sentiments about it. Even her mother enjoyed a good game of football, and often made a load of snacks for the street to enjoy while Ruby watched on in amazement as a bunch of people who rarely spoke came together in food and football.

The cheerleaders were the first to leave.

Several of them took one look at her and giggled. She couldn't stand it when they did that. Next, a few of the team left. Again, a couple looked her way and smirked. Did it look like she was hanging out here waiting for Theo when he was the one to ask her on a date?

She pushed the doubt aside, and she didn't have to wait much longer for Theo.

He walked out with Mike, who she knew was his best friend.

The moment Theo saw her, he stepped right up to her. "I was worried you wouldn't come. I didn't see you at the game."

"I've been studying. Mom just dropped me off."

Mike approached, and she sensed the awkwardness of the moment.

"You two coming to the party?"

"Nah, we're out of here. See you tomorrow? Practice?" Theo said.

"You practice on a weekend?" she asked.

"Mike comes to my place. We take some practice shots and tackles, that kind of thing."

"Oh, right. Sounds fun." She tucked some hair behind her ear. She wondered, not for the first time, if she should have put it up.

"You don't have to pretend. I know sports isn't your thing. You look beautiful," Theo said. He held out his hand, and her heart sped up. "You ready?"

She wanted to scream that she was so not ready for any of this.

She took his hand. He was so much bigger than

she was. Large, football hands.

Interesting.

They walked toward his car, and he held open the door and she slid inside. Her cell phone was inside her pocket so if anything bad happened, her mother was a phone call away. Callie had already told her she'd buy ice cream for them to talk for when she got home. This was why she loved her mom. Callie always knew what she needed even before she realized it.

Theo dumped his bag into the trunk before climbing behind the wheel. His car wasn't flashy, or an up-to-date model.

Again, she didn't really know anything about cars.

They pulled out of the parking lot, and he pressed on his horn, giving his teammates a wave before they left.

"Did you win?" she asked.

"You really want to know?"

"Of course. I wouldn't be able to understand the game or anything, but I hope you won."

"Hell, yeah, we did. The crowd was going wild."

"Cool." She smiled.

"I see that look. Are you interested yet in watching a football game at all?"

"Nope. It doesn't appeal really, but if you want me to, I will. You'll have to tell me everything that is going on, but I can learn."

"We'll leave that for now. What do you like to do for fun? Besides studying."

"Come on, studying can be fun. Just think about the future you want and realize it all depends on how well you do in high school. You get the best colleges wanting your ass, and you move up in this world. Easy."

"College is important to you?" he asked.

"It is. Especially for what I want." She didn't tell him what she wanted to become.

"Your dad went to a good college, didn't he?"

She didn't like talking about her dad but saw there was no point in avoiding it. "He did."

"I'm sorry about him leaving you."

She chuckled. "It was a long time ago."

"I'm nervous. I don't know what to say to you."

"You're nervous?"

"Yeah, why wouldn't I be?"

"You're one of the most popular guys in school and you're nervous."

"I'm with a girl I really, really want to impress. Yeah, I'm nervous."

She stared down at her thighs. She liked that he was nervous. It was a good thing for him to be nervous, right?

"I'm nervous too. I've never been on a date before."

"You haven't?"

"You're the first guy to ask me and for me to accept."

"You've been asked before. You have to be."

"Why?" she asked.

"You're beautiful, smart. You've got this incredible smile that won't let any guy look away."

She leaned her head back on the chair and looked at him. He didn't seem to be speaking bullshit or trying to string her along. "You're sweet."

"I'm speaking the truth. That's all I can do."

Chapter Three

The pizza parlor was incredibly busy when they entered. The moment the locals saw him, they started to talk about the game. They waited in line, and he wasn't willing to be rude to the team's fans. Theo had no illusions they were *his* fans. It was all about the school football team, and he was merely on it.

However, he didn't like that Ruby kept getting ignored.

Talking with her was so easy, even with her nerves, and so much fun. He loved listening to her as she spoke and of course, making her laugh.

It was a date.

He'd made sure she was aware of them being together, together. So, while one guy was talking about one of the shots he made, he wrapped his arm around Ruby, drawing her close.

She looked ready to run off at any minute.

The guy, who he believed ran the hardware store, seemed to take the hint, finished his point, and got back in line.

"What are you doing?" she asked.

"I'm making sure everyone knows I'm here on a date."

"You really have to make a show of it like this?"

"Do you *want* me to talk about football all night?" he asked, watching her.

"If that's what you want to do."

He smiled. "And you could brand this the worst date ever. Not happening."

"It wouldn't be a terrible date. Just one I don't understand."

The line soon got down, and he ordered himself a pepperoni. Ruby asked for the same, and they both waited for their order to be ready. There was a small booth in the back, and he kept eyeing it, hoping no one took it.

Their pizza didn't take long, and he was more than happy to be given the hot wings, free of charge.

No one took the booth, and carrying their food over, he waited for Ruby to slide in. The booth had a round table, but only had one way of getting in and out. By making sure Ruby sat on the other side of him, she couldn't escape.

"You're a celebrity in this town," she said.

"You know that already."

"True." She took a piece of pizza, and he watched her take a large bite. He and a bunch of the team had come to the pizza parlor with the cheerleading squad. Most of them chewed their way through a salad, never once touching the pizza. He often found it sad. Pizza, with all the gooey melting cheese and assortment of toppings, was the best thing in the world. "Have I got cheese on my chin?" She wiped at her face.

"No, you're perfect."

"You keep staring."

"I enjoy spending time with you."

"You know, this date is not going the way I thought it would."

"It's only just started, but I'm intrigued. How did you think it would go?"

"I don't know. You'd talk about nothing but football. Stuff like that. I judged you even before I got here. I'm sorry about that."

He rolled his eyes, playfully. "Don't worry about it. The only thing I want to talk about is you."

"I'm not good with talking about myself. Besides, you've got me curious about you, Theo West, star player, who wants to date me. So, what are your plans for the future?" she asked.

"Ugh, don't you get sick and tired of people asking that?" He was growing tired of his parents, the counselors, teachers, all of them wanting to have a suitable answer.

"Agreed. My mom is the best though. She told me to let her know my plans and she'd work around them."

"You love your mom?"

"Totally. She's the best. She's a rock, even after everything with my dad. I know she still misses him at times, but she's never once let me down."

"She sounds amazing. Maybe one day I could meet her," Theo offered.

"That's a giant leap from one date, right? Meeting a parent?"

"You can meet both of mine. I don't mind."

"Theo, what's really going on here? Aren't guys supposed to be terrified at the idea of meeting parents?"

"You've clearly watched too many movies. I want to go on a date with you. Actually, scrap that, many dates. Lots of dates."

"No, that's impossible." She took a bite of pizza, but couldn't help but smile.

"Why is that impossible?" He reached out, pushing a curl of hair off her face.

She didn't push him away, but he didn't press for more. Taking another slice of pizza, he waited.

"You're supposed to enjoy being the party animal. Sleeping with random girls. Doing crazy stuff that no other eighteen-year-old should want to do, but wish they could. You could get away with everything."

He chuckled. "You think I'm a crazy jock?"

"Aren't you?" she asked.

He sucked on the straw of his drink, waiting.

"First, you really need to watch a whole lot of different movies. I think I should start over. I'm Theo West. I'm a football player. A really good one. I also get straight As in all of my classes, and I'm not looking to get a football scholarship, but I wouldn't mind because I love the game. I'm not obsessed with it. I do enjoy horror movies and hard rock music, which drives my family crazy. I enjoy spy novels, and while we're at it, I make a mean lasagna. It's the only thing I can cook, and whenever my family gets sick, I tend to cook it for them even though they can't eat it. Also, I like you, Ruby James. A lot. A whole lot. So much so that I decided to break the mold of my football lifestyle and take you on a date. I'd love for this to work, even though you are being somewhat judgmental. I will grant you, I love looking at your ass and have been admiring it for years." He finished with a bite of his pizza.

Ruby was red-faced. "Oh."

"I'm not just some dumb jock now, huh?"

"No, you're not."

"Want to kiss my cheek in apology?"

She shook her head. "No, I'll give you the same." He watched her take a deep breath, and he didn't even check her tits out. A giant leap forward for him. "I'm Ruby James. I guess you can say I'm a bit of a nerd. I like eating lunch in the library and studying. I have good grades. A couple of As and Bs but nothing too bad. My dad left when I was young, and he does keep in touch, but I find it hard to communicate with him for what he did. I've never been on a single date before. I love romance. You can mock if you wish, but you'll never get another date out of me. Also, I like pop music and country. I've never listened to a single heavy metal song, and I cook with my mom. We have several days in one month where we make things in advance, so we don't have to order takeout. This is the first pizza I've ever eaten that wasn't my mom's. Also, I don't think you're a dumb jock, not anymore."

"See, turned your thoughts around in one date. How is it?" he asked.

"How's what?"

"The pizza?"

"It's good but not as good as hers." He watched her swallow some more. "Maybe one day, if we're still dating, you can come and try some."

"Now that, I'd like."

Progress.

****

Three hours later

It was late, but tomorrow was the weekend. The main light was still on so Ruby knew her mother was waiting. Their date was … amazing. They ate pizza, and after they shared pieces of themselves, it seemed to go a lot easier.

Theo stopped the car outside of her house, leaving the engine running.

"I actually had a really nice time."

He'd taken her stargazing. They had sat on the hood of his car, on a blanket, and he pointed out each of the stars. He also brought with him some binoculars to make it easier for her to see. She loved the date. Much to her surprise, he was very romantic.

Now though, her nerves were back.

End of date jitters.

"I want to take you out again," he said.

"You do?"

"Yeah. How about next Friday? We don't have a game, and we can, I don't know, go to the mall."

"The mall?"

"There's a movie place. They're playing

something good, I'm sure. Not for stereotypical jock types either."

"I don't mind the movies. How about going paintballing?"

"You'd like to do that?"

"Hell, yeah, it's always a lot of fun. I've gone with my mom a few times. I love it. You can shoot at me and teach me sports."

"Consider it a date."

"I will."

Theo reached out, stroking her cheek. She didn't know what to do. His gaze went from her eyes to her lips, then back. Ruby knew what he wanted, but she also knew she couldn't exactly give in to him. Not yet.

"Erm, I better go." She pulled out of his hold, and climbed out of the car.

"Ruby, wait."

She stopped on her front steps, waiting. "What is it?"

"Look, I was just going to kiss you."

"I'm not ready for that."

"Okay. I can wait. Whenever you're comfortable, I can wait. You still don't trust me."

"It's not that. Please, don't think that. It's a lot to take in, and it's like, wow. You're blowing my mind right now, Theo. A kiss is … it has to mean something. I don't know. I don't go around kissing random guys."

"Then these lips are for you when you're ready. Can I coax a cheek kiss from you?"

"A cheek kiss?"

"Yes."

He took her hands. She tensed up as he moved in close. His lips grazed her cheek. "A cheek kiss, nothing more. I had a wonderful night, Ruby." She watched as he stepped back. "I'll wait for you to go in."

"Oh, right." She pulled out her key, unlocking her front door. She turned to him and gave him a wave. "Goodnight."

"Goodnight."

Closing the door, she flicked the lock and stared at her mother, who was waiting, arms folded, against the doorframe.

"I like that smile."

"Mom?"

"I got ice cream, and it's ready for us. Go, get changed. Tell me all about it."

Her mother rushed her upstairs, and Ruby took a quick shower before changing into a pair of pajamas. She found four different ice cream flavors waiting for her.

"All of these looked amazing, and I didn't want us to go without. It's not every single day my only daughter goes on a date. What do you want?"

"I'll take the chocolate," she said.

"Good." Her mother didn't scoop out ice cream. No, she handed her the tub, and Ruby loved her even more for it.

"Tell me every single part."

She told her mother everything. From the pizza, to their talk, and then the stargazing, plans for the future, and then the kiss.

"Why didn't you let him kiss you?"

"I don't know. I mean, I do, but it's stupid."

"Come on. I'm your mother. You can tell me everything."

"I wonder if you'd be this cool when I have sex."

"I'd like to think I'll be."

Ruby chuckled. "Fine. Fine. I've never been kissed before in my life. You and Dad don't count. Neither do any of my teddies or anything that is not breathing."

"You kissed a tree once, that was breathing."

"I was five, and again, doesn't count. Please, don't ever mention that."

"You fell in love with trees. It's sweet and cute."

"It's weird."

"Not for me." Her mother smirked. "I get it. Your father was the only guy I kissed throughout high school."

"Do you hate him?"

"No."

"Why not? He just got up and left."

"I know, but it was time for him to leave. I know you'll never understand it, but your father and I, we work the way we do."

"You're dating him?"

"No. He calls often asking about you. We talk. It works for us, especially now. He wants to be involved in your future."

She didn't know her parents talked.

"When are you going to move on?" Ruby asked.

"When I'm good and ready. You know me, honey. I'm happy the way I am."

"I know. It's what scares me."

Her mother smiled. "I can meddle in my daughter's life, just fine. I like the sound of this boy."

"I promised him you'd make him some pizza if we were still dating."

"I've got a feeling you will be," Callie said.

"Why?"

"Just a hunch is all." Her mother winked at her. "Enjoy your ice cream while it's still cold."

Chapter Four

Theo: **I loved spending time with you.**
Ruby: **I did too. You're not so bad.**
Theo: **You looking forward to next week?**
Ruby: **School or date?**
Theo: **Both.**
Ruby: **School.**
Theo: **I'll make you pay for that.**
Ruby: **I'm so afraid.**
Theo: **We'll see.**
Ruby: **I look forward to seeing you.**

Theo couldn't wipe the smile off his face as he waited for Ruby to make an appearance in school. He'd arrived early to get everything he needed from his locker. Now, he stood outside of the school with his buddies, but he was waiting for Ruby to arrive. Her car parking space was still clear. He checked the time and saw she still had ten minutes to arrive.

He'd wanted to go and see her over the weekend, but Mike convinced him to give her time.

All he'd allowed himself were a few texts.

"You're acting so uncool right now. I think we should kick you off the team."

"Screw you."

"You know the cheerleaders are mega pissed at you."

"Why?"

"You've got a thing for a different chick. An outsider and they don't like it."

Theo smiled as he watched Ruby pull into the parking spot. "Look at my face, dude. It doesn't give a fuck." He slapped Mike on the back and walked over to the girl on his mind. Opening the door for her, he bent down. "Morning, beautiful."

"What are you doing?"

"You're always so cynical. I thought that was supposed to happen in old age."

"I've aged before my time."

"How old are you?" he asked.

"I'm sixty."

"You're a hot piece of ass for sixty."

She laughed. "Wow, you have a way with words."

"You bring out the natural poet in me."

She climbed out of the car, taking the door from him and closing it.

"Happy Monday," he said.

"What are you doing?"

"I'm proving to you that Friday was no trick, and I happen to enjoy spending time with you." He stroked a finger down her arm, and without giving her a chance to pull away, he locked their fingers together. "See, not afraid for people to see."

"I've got to go to my locker." She tried to pull her hand away, but he wouldn't let her. She stopped fighting him with a giggle. "Look, I know you want me to just relax about all this, but it's really hard to do. I'm not trying to be a bitch. I've just got to get used to this."

"You will. I won't give you a reason not to. Let's go."

Walking across the parking lot, he saw guys and girls watching them. He made sure they could all see him holding her hand, so they wouldn't doubt who she belonged to.

When he glanced over at Mike, his best friend smirked at him. He also checked the cheerleaders, and yes, they looked pissed. He didn't care.

Ruby was his, and he'd already wasted so much time in not asking her out. He wasn't willing to let that time go again.

"You know people are staring?"

"Yes."

"You don't care."

"No."

"I do."

"Don't let them win. I want to date you. I don't want to do this in secret." They stopped off at her locker. "So, I'm going to date you."

She paused with her fingers on the dial. "Do you mean date or become, like, a couple? A couple means a lot more dates."

He smiled. "I want you to be my girlfriend."

"That's a step up from dating."

"That's the logical progression that two people who date, do. They become a couple. Boyfriend and girlfriend."

"You've thought about this a lot."

"I figured you'd argue what I wanted."

"So we're a couple now?"

"Yes. Boyfriend and girlfriend."

"We don't kiss."

"We don't have to. Boyfriend and girlfriend who are currently in the first day of their brand-new relationship."

She twisted the dial, and he could see her brain working. When the lock didn't give, he took over, slamming his fist three times against the door, and it popped open.

"See, boyfriend material."

"I see." She released her bag and kept on watching him.

"What?"

"I'm just trying to figure out what you want from me. I've never been a girlfriend, and this is a new development from stargazing."

"First, I've never had a girlfriend either. We're both new to all of this. Secondly, you're the only person I've ever taken to see the stars and talked about them. Third, I like you. I'm a West. I'm taught to go after everything I want in life."

"And you've decided you want me."

"Yes. I also know, I'll be good for you."

"Why?"

"Look at me, baby. I'm awesome."

This made her laugh, and he loved the sound.

"Okay, so what does that mean for me?"

"You can't sneak off to the library anymore. Your ass has to sit beside me at the cafeteria."

"No, come on. It's so quiet in the library."

"I could bring all the guys to the library. That would be fun."

"No, no, no. We'll work it out." She grabbed a few books, slamming her locker closed. "Next one?"

"I get to walk you to class. Holding your hand for all the world to see. You're going to also have to come to a few games. Don't worry, I'll teach you when to cheer. You can even bring a book if you'd like."

"This is going to be exhausting."

"But fun. Never forget that. Totally fun. So much fun. Here we arrive at your first destination." He lifted up their hands and kissed her knuckles. "I'll be seeing you soon."

"How did you know my first class?" she asked.

"I know a lot of things, and I've got a way of finding them out." He wasn't about to spill all of his secrets. Leaning in, he brushed his lips against her cheek. "I'll respect your boundaries until you're ready for my lips on yours. FYI, you're going to love my kisses."

With that, he pulled away, offered her a wink,

and left.

Being a boyfriend was actually a lot of fun.

****

Ruby didn't know if being a girlfriend was something she was cut out for. Sure, she loved him holding her hand, and got a buzz out of being escorted to her first class, but … the stares. Even when he wasn't around, girls were talking behind their cupped hands, and they didn't even make a show of trying to hide the fact they were talking about her.

She wasn't fucking stupid!

She knew who they were talking about.

By the time lunch came, she wasn't surprised to see Theo waiting for her, standing by her locker with that smirk on his lips.

"Hey, girlfriend. How is your day going?"

"Crappy. Yours, boyfriend?" She winced, not sure if calling him a boyfriend would work for her, but it did sound good though.

"It's been awesome. I'm off the market. I've had five chicks ask me out, and I've been able to turn each of them down flat."

He slammed his fist against her locker.

"You're not sad about that?"

"Why would I be sad? I've got a girlfriend."

"They will kiss you and probably do other things with you."

He shrugged. "I don't want to kiss just anyone. Besides, I can handle a cheek." He leaned in close and kissed her cheek. "See, I like this. I like our boundaries. I can respect your wishes."

"Why?"

"I like you." He held his hand out. "Now, your turn."

"I can't stand people talking about me."

"Ah, yes, I've heard. Some people think you're pregnant."

"What? How could they think that with one date?"

"I don't know. They like to make up shit as they go along." He held her hand all the way to the cafeteria.

She made him halt at the doors.

"What is it?" he asked.

"I don't know if I can go in there."

"Well, I can. No one is going to point or say shit while I'm with you."

"I don't think my life should be controlled by your mere presence, Theo." She tried to pull her hand away, but again, he wouldn't let her.

"You know, I thought you were above what other people thought of you."

"I am."

"Then why do you even care what they think? We had an amazing date. Are you really going to let a bunch of kids tell you what you can and cannot do?"

"No, of course not."

"Good. Me neither."

He pulled her into the cafeteria, and they went straight to the lunch line. Theo grabbed her hips and stood behind her.

She held the tray, and he rested his chin on her head.

"What looks good today, do you think?" he asked.

"Not the coleslaw." She wrinkled her nose.

"You heard the rumors about all the staff spitting into it whenever one of us pisses them off?"

"Are you willing to risk it?"

"I don't eat coleslaw. I don't like raw cabbage."

"Interesting."

He hummed his approval. "Anything you don't like?"

"Guys holding my hips and moving me down the line?" She giggled.

"Don't worry, I'll make sure they stop. That way, I'm the only one doing it. Since I'm your boyfriend, I get touching hip rights." He gave her hips a squeeze. "And you like it."

"You're insane."

"Only for you."

They both settled on a couple of burgers and fries.

Her home had a power outage during the night, so her alarm didn't go off, and she'd slept in, making it impossible for her to grab lunch from home. She'd had to leave straight away to arrive in time for school.

She hated cafeteria food, but she couldn't be choosy today.

Theo wouldn't let her pay. When they got to the lunch lady at the register he pulled out his wallet and paid for their food. Then, with his hands back on her hips, he walked her across the hall to his table. The guys were in shock, she could clearly see it, but they didn't say a word, instead making room for the two of them. Theo made sure she sat down first before taking a seat beside her.

"Everyone, you know Ruby. Ruby, you know everyone."

She held her hand up, feeling completely out of place. "Hey, everyone."

"You two are a thing now? It's not just a rumor?" Jake asked.

Ruby didn't bother answering.

"She's my exclusive girlfriend. You got a problem with it, take it up with me."

"He likes to throw around the girlfriend word a lot," she said, taking her burger.

"How long you been going out?" David asked.

They were all members of the football team, and she hated all the questions.

Theo didn't seem to mind and took them all in stride. "Since Friday."

"We've been official boyfriend and girlfriend since this morning," she said, popping in a fry.

"Wow, you work fast."

She didn't catch who said that.

"Are you pregnant?"

She turned to Mike, knowing he was Theo's best friend.

"No."

"How can you be so sure?" another guy asked.

"Enough," Theo said.

She was growing tired of all the questions. "Have you ever attended sex ed?" she asked.

"Yeah."

"Then you know you've got to actually do something to get pregnant, right?"

"You're saying you and Theo haven't done anything?" David asked.

She raised her brow and glanced at Theo.

Her brand-new boyfriend was smirking. "What's the matter, David?"

"I just can't imagine you being a boyfriend without getting laid."

"Well, I can't imagine you playing ball whenever you're on the bench."

That stopped David from laughing.

"Ruby's my girlfriend. She's not to be made fun of, and you're sure as shit not to be spreading rumors. You hear anything, you nip it in the bud," Theo said.

She was surprised by his support and how serious he sounded as well.

"Why the fuck should we do that?" Jake asked.

"As your friend and as your captain, I'm asking you to make sure my girlfriend is taken care of, or are we only a team on the field?" Theo asked.

"You know we'll take care of her and you," Mike said.

Her heart pounded as one by one, the guys agreed. She couldn't believe Theo would do that.

Staring at him now, she was a little ... shocked. This time, she kissed his cheek and smiled.

"What was that for?"

"I think that's one of the sweetest things you could have done."

The table erupted in ahs at her.

Her face went red, but Theo didn't seem to care.

"I take care of what's mine."

"I'm not property."

"I know you're not, but to these guys, you're mine. I won't have you feeling like shit around this school because I want to be your boyfriend. I'm proving to you this is not a trick. I'm not bullshitting you. I mean what I say."

She was starting to get that about Theo.

Chapter Five

Ten more dates ensued over the next month. They were not only on a Friday but also a Saturday, and even through the week. Theo loved spending time with Ruby, as he knew he would.

Tonight, he'd be meeting her mother, and he knew she was nervous and saw it in her eyes when he walked to her locker later that day. She was gathering her books, and he took the bag from her, never wanting her to carry something so heavy. It had taken a month, but no one was shocked anymore to see them together.

"Are you sure you want to do this?"

"Your mom's pizza night is supposed to be epic. What kind of boyfriend would I be if I didn't invite myself?"

"A sane one. I thought all boyfriends were supposed to be afraid to meet the parent."

"They are, but I think this one will be cool." He took her hand, and they walked out of high school together. His friends thought he was crazy, especially as they knew he still wasn't getting any. Not that he told them, they just seemed to know.

Theo didn't care what anyone thought.

He liked that he was having to work for it, that she wasn't willing to have sex straight away, giving them both a chance to get to know one another.

Chasing after Ruby wasn't about fucking her. She was different from other girls, and he certainly wasn't about to ruin his chance with her for a quick fuck.

He'd picked her up from her house that morning, so he was driving them both. He'd offered to wear his uniform, but Ruby wasn't impressed. She never fawned all over him when he wore it.

"Are there any topics you think I should avoid?"

Theo asked.

"None. My mom's a pretty open book. She's cool about everything. I wouldn't worry so much."

"She sounds awesome."

"I'm biased. I do think she is awesome, but you never know, I may see a whole new side to her with you."

"You're not helping."

She chuckled. "I like this," she said.

"What?"

"Being with you. Hanging out. Having fun."

"Wait until we upgrade to the kissing part."

She rolled her eyes, and he had no choice but to focus on the road.

The moment they pulled up outside of her house, he noticed Ruby tense up.

"What is it?"

"I don't know." She unbuckled her seatbelt, and he had no choice but to follow her out.

Walking up the drive, he noticed how upset she was. She pulled out her key, opening the door.

"Mom, I'm home. I brought Theo with me."

In the past month, he'd never known her to react like this.

She wouldn't budge past the door. There was enough room for him to close it behind him, and then he turned to see the lady from the veterinary clinic where he'd gotten his dog, Scooch, dealt with after he ate chocolate he shouldn't have done. Of course, he also knew Callie for another reason, but he wasn't going to spill the beans on that little secret.

Beside Callie was a man, and Theo recognized him, even though he'd not been around town for a long time.

"What is this?" Ruby asked.

"Ruby!"

"Honey, hello, sweetie," he said.

Theo placed a hand on her back, offering her comfort as he got a sense she really needed it in that moment.

"You okay?" he asked.

"This is your boyfriend," Callie said, smiling.

He noticed Ruby hadn't looked away from her father.

After a few seconds, she seemed to shake herself out of it. "Mom, this is Theo. Theo, this is my mom, Callie James."

He shook her hand as he didn't know what else to do. Turning to the guy, he waited another few awkward moments.

"This is my dad."

She didn't offer any name, and still, he shook his head, getting a sense he really didn't want to get involved.

"Why's he here?" Ruby asked, turning to her mother.

Shoving his hands back in his pockets, Theo really didn't know what to say.

"Honey, he's your father."

"He left eight years ago."

"And now I'm back," he said.

"What's going on? You're just going to allow him to come back here? All is forgiven?"

"Sweetheart, we never actually got divorced, and he owns the house, and we've been trying to keep things amicable for you."

"Wow, I can't—"

"How about we sit down and have some pizza?" Ruby's dad said. "I think that's good for everyone, and we can just relax and get to know each other."

"I need to go and put my bag in my room." She grabbed Theo's hand, and he saw her dad looking ready to attack him.

"You're not taking a boy to your room."

"Theo's my boyfriend. We're not going to do anything. Besides, you're not the boss of me."

"Ruby!"

They were gone before they could be stopped.

Within seconds, he was inside Ruby's bedroom, and one look around her room, he knew it was hers. The color scheme was so light and bright. Pictures filled one wall, from family to scenic views.

"Sorry about that," she said.

"Hey, I didn't think for a second seeing your dad would get me into your room."

"It's nothing. I'm sorry. I've not seen him in a really long time."

"Eight years?"

"Pretty much. I wasn't interested in visiting him in the city. Mom didn't want to drive me out. He didn't want to come and pick me up. I like where I live so never saw a reason to change. I was a bitch down there, wasn't I?"

Theo sat down on the edge of her bed. "You're asking my advice?"

"You're supposed to be meeting my mother, and it's turned into a mini drama."

"It's nothing that we can't handle."

She tucked her hair behind her ear, smiling. "We?"

"You got that right, we." He held out his hands, and she took them. "I don't know everything that went on down there well enough to tell you if you were a bitch or not. It's not my place."

He grabbed her ass, holding her close. He hugged

her, and she ran her fingers through his hair. He loved the touch, the gentleness of her fingers on him.

His cock started to harden at the merest caress from her.

She suddenly pulled back and smiled at him. Seconds later, her lips were on his, in their first real kiss.

****

Ruby's lips still tingled as she sat at the table, very aware of her father near her. Theo sat opposite her while her parents were on either side of the table.

"So, your mother tells me you've already got your letters and packages ready for the colleges you want to attend next year."

She stared at her mother's pizza on the plate, and anger simmered inside. Why did he have to come back now?

One glance at Callie, and she looked fine. It pissed Ruby off.

"Don't ignore him, sweetheart," Callie said.

"I don't get this," Ruby said, looking between both of her parents. "He just got up and left. I mean, why is he even here?"

"He wanted to come and see you. We know it has been a long time, and we didn't want to rush you."

"I still love your mother. We have been through a difficult time," he said.

Ruby shook her head. "No, that is not possible. People who love each other don't go to the big city to get a job and never turn back up."

"Honey, he did turn back up. You just weren't here when he did. It was only the one time, but we've been building … bridges. I did send divorce papers, and that's when he came back, not too long ago," Callie said.

Ruby got to her feet. "I don't want to hear this."

Stepping back from the table, she didn't stop

when her parents told her to. Theo was right behind her, and she was in his car, not looking back at the house.

"You want me to go?" he asked.

"Yes, please. I don't want to be at home right now."

He pulled away from her house, and she didn't even look back.

"You're not the biggest fan of your dad."

"I believe my mom deserves someone a lot better than him."

"Okay." Theo kept on driving until they arrived at his home. She'd never been inside, and there was no sign of any cars. "My parents are away for the weekend."

"Oh."

"If you're not comfortable…"

"Yes, yes, I'm fine." Climbing out of the car, she followed him into his home.

Once inside, she saw how homey it was. There were jackets hung up in the hall, and she saw shoes aligned against the wall. The next thing she noticed were all the pictures of them. His family. She'd not met them, but she'd seen them on his cell phone when he shared them.

It looked amazing.

One day, she hoped to have a big family.

"Your mom's pizza was cool."

She tucked her hair behind her ears, and nodded. "Yeah, very cool."

"I'm going to go and shower."

Ruby turned to him. "So, I get to see your room?"

"We're all about sharing today." He held out his hand, and she took it.

She loved holding his hand and that kiss. She didn't even know what came over her. His lips had been like a magnet, begging for her to kiss, and she'd given in, and explored his mouth. Theo had reciprocated and kissed her back, making her breathless.

When the kiss had ended, she'd not wanted to go downstairs but to keep on kissing him.

His bedroom was a real man cave.

Football trophies were on one wall, along with pictures and newspaper cutouts. "My dad thinks it's important for me to be surrounded in positivity."

"You should. This is your achievement, and it's amazing, Theo. Don't ever let anyone tell you otherwise." She stepped up to the board.

"You like them?"

"They're part of you, so yeah, I like them."

"You're admitting you're liking me?"

"I do like you."

Theo wrapped his arms around her, kissing her neck. "I know you don't get sports."

"I get them. I just don't agree with them, but that's not going to stop me from liking you. I'm also listening and I'm starting to learn the rules, so one day I'll know if you're doing a good pass or a bad one."

"One day you'll come and watch a game and you'll see." He kissed her again. "I've got to go and head for a shower. I stink."

She laughed.

There was a television in the corner, and cupboards across one wall with a few books on top and his deodorant.

Sitting on the edge of the bed, she took everything in, feeling comfortable. This was Theo's room. His domain. His cave.

She liked it. It suited him, even the cream walls and black furniture.

It wasn't long before he returned with a towel wrapped around his waist. His body was on full display, every hard, muscular inch of him.

"You okay?"

"Yeah. I just realized that I'm alone in a room with you and you're naked."

"You worried I'll take advantage?"

She shook her head.

"What is it?" he asked, stepping in front of her.

"I'm worried I'll take advantage of you."

He laughed. "I hate to break this to you, but I've got no problem being taken advantage of."

She stood up. Her hands went to his hips, holding him steady as she stared into his eyes.

Something was happening right now, and as she leaned in to kiss him, she didn't want to stop. Slowly, she ran her hand up his chest, watching him as he circled his neck.

Was she ready? Could she do this?

Theo wrapped his arm around her, and she waited, watching him.

With her other hand, she fingered the edge of his towel, toying with it.

"What are you doing?"

"I really like you, Theo. I know I've been … weird, and I'm sorry. I just, I'm not used to being wanted."

"I want you."

"I like that you want me, and I want you."

"What are you saying, Ruby?

She dropped the towel but didn't look at him. She stayed in his arms, watching him.

"I'm ready, Theo," she said.

Finding his erection, she wrapped her fingers around his length, and waited.

"I want you."

It was the only time she'd ever said it, and this

would be her very first time. She was ready, and she wanted him.

Chapter Six

At first, Theo didn't know what to do. With Ruby's hand on him, he couldn't even think. This was what he'd been wanting for so long, and now it was finally here, he was freaking out while keeping it together.

He wasn't a virgin. That ship had sailed a long time ago. His first time had meant nothing to him.

Gripping her hand on his cock, he stared into her eyes.

"Ruby, no, you don't want this."

"I do want this."

"This is about your father."

"No, this is about the two of us. I'm ready, Theo. I want you. No one else." She kissed him again, and he was completely lost. "If you don't want to, we'll stop."

"I don't want you to feel pressured."

"I feel like I'm the one doing all the pressuring."

He cupped the back of her neck and showed her with actions how he truly felt. He hardened the kiss, wanting to taste her, exploring her mouth, moaning as she opened up to him and he could deepen the kiss.

Her hand still worked on his dick, but he didn't even try to push her away. He stepped toward the bed, pushing her down. She lay back, and he stared down at her after breaking from the kiss.

Taking hold of her hand, he lifted it above her head.

"I'm the one in charge if we do this."

"I've got a feeling you have a lot more experience than me."

Touching her hip, he lifted up her shirt and leaned down to press kisses along her stomach.

She let out a gasp, arching up, and he continued

to trail kisses as he exposed her to his gaze. Removing her shirt completely, he made quick work of her bra, and her tits were incredible. He'd spent a great deal of time admiring them and wanting them. Seeing them now, he was completely floored by her beauty. She truly was stunning.

His cock hardened even more, and he couldn't get enough of her.

Dropping a kiss to each peaked tip, he flicked his tongue across, and relished her gasp as he did.

He sat back, working the catch of her jeans, and together, they slid them off her body, and before he had any doubts, he removed her panties as well. She lay beneath him, open, spread out, for his gaze only.

Stroking her thighs, he slowly drew his fingers up, moving toward her center and touching her pussy.

She gasped.

Moving down the bed so his mouth was above her, he spread her lips wide, and licked between her slit.

She cried out his name, and he loved the taste of her. Up and down he slid his tongue, feeling the shock slowly leave her body as she started to rock against his face. Sucking her clit into his mouth, he used his teeth to bite down just slightly, hearing her cry out before soothing out that pain with his tongue.

Staring up the length of her body, he watched her tits shake. His own cock was begging for him to touch. The past month, in fact, the past year he'd been wanting her, he'd had blue balls.

This for him, was a dream come true. To finally have her in his bed, giving her pleasure was what he'd been wanting for so long now.

Over and over he suckled on her clit, wanting to take her virginity, but holding back.

When she came, he wished he could see her face

and watch her come apart. There would be time for that. He waited for her orgasm to ebb away before moving up her body and staring down into her eyes.

She looked mesmerized, and he was completely drawn to her. He reached into his drawer and got a condom.

"Are you sure you're ready?"

"Yes. I'm ready."

He tore into the condom, sliding it over his erection and moving between her spread legs. His nerves took over as he stared at her. She meant everything to him. For so long now, he'd been trying to get with this girl, and the past month had been a whirlwind.

She wasn't some joke or a passing fancy.

Ruby was the woman he wanted to be with.

With his cock at her entrance, he knew it was going to hurt. In one swift, hard, thrust, he filled her pussy, tearing through her virginity and claiming her as his own.

Once it was done, he kissed away her cries and wiped away her tears, keeping himself perfectly still within her, not wanting to cause her any more pain. He didn't know how long the pain lasted for, only that he didn't want to hear her cry like that again.

When no more tears fell, he lifted up, and stared down into her eyes.

"You okay?" he asked and winced.

"Yes. I knew there'd be pain."

"I didn't want to prolong it."

"You had sex with a lot of virgins?"

"None." He stroked her cheek. "Just you."

"Just me?"

"Yeah, and only you from now on."

"Theo?"

"Don't say anything. I know you doubt me at

every turn, but there's no need to. I'm not going to hurt you, but that's okay. I will spend every single waking moment of my life to prove to you that I'll never hurt you. That I'm here. I have no reason to leave. You're everything that I want." When he finished, he pulled out of her, and slowly began to sink inside her.

She gasped.

He thrust inside slowly, feeling the walls of her pussy tighten around him, gripping him.

Waiting for her to belong to him was the best time he'd ever spent. Over and over, he thrust, making love to her. Kissing her lips, he couldn't believe she was his, and he certainly had no intention of ever giving her up, not for anything.

Driving in deep, he felt the first pulse of his own arousal. After months of going without, and finally being in the woman he wanted, he filled the condom, feeling like he was drowning in a sea of need.

Ruby arched up, screaming his name, and he felt her release as well with him. They came together, and to Theo, it was the best experience of his life.

****

The condom had broken.

Ruby watched as Theo disposed of it, returning to his bedroom with a washcloth. She was no longer a virgin. She had sex after walking out on her parents. Her life couldn't get any more complicated, and yet, the condom had broken.

On their first time.

He wiped away the remnants of his semen and her virgin blood, leaving her again before returning. Theo didn't grab his clothes.

He climbed into bed, wrapping his arms around her and holding her close.

Neither of them spoke for what felt like a

lifetime.

Were words really needed?

"The condom broke."

"Did you enjoy that?"

They both talked at the same time.

Ruby smiled. "Yes, I enjoyed it."

"We'll handle whatever happens. Do you want me to try and find the morning after pill?" Theo asked.

"You'd do that?" She looked up at him.

"I'd do anything for you."

"Really?"

Theo opened his mouth and closed it.

"What?" she asked. "What is it?"

"I, erm, I'd met your mother before today. Before you introduced us."

"I know. She told me that she remembered you and your dog. Where is your dog?"

"My parents take him with them whenever they have to leave the house, so he's not on his own with me at school and everything."

"Ah, I'd love to meet him."

"I asked your mother for help."

"What?" Ruby asked, watching him.

"The day at the vet. I knew who she was, and in all honesty, I was getting desperate."

"Desperate for what?"

"To get to know you. To talk to you. I couldn't think of how best to get your attention, and I told your mother."

"Wait. My mom knew you were going to ask me out?" Ruby asked.

"Yes. I told her I had very deep feelings for you, and she asked me how deep, and I told her the truth. You mother really should work for law enforcement or something."

"You have feelings for me?"

Theo cupped her cheek. "How could you think I don't?"

"Theo, you don't think this is moving too fast?"

He laughed. "I'm in love with you."

Her heart pounded. "What?"

"I told your mother that. I knew without a doubt my feelings for you, and at first, she laughed at me. Told me that I didn't know what I was talking about. Then, I told her what I felt. How I watched you from afar and had been doing so all these years. How you went through that year of wearing nothing but dungarees all year with a different neon shirt. She told me you were going through your rebel stage. I thought you looked so cute, and I loved the way they hugged your ass. Then you went in long dresses. Another thing you were going through. I didn't like them. They were always too big and never showed your curves, apart from when you walked with speed. I'd watch you during classes, at lunch when you were around. I saw you around town with your mom, and I even begged my parents for a dog. We went to the rescue, so I could go to the vet's."

Tears filled her eyes as he continued.

"For a long time, I've been wanting to be part of your life. To see you smile. To watch you, but I didn't know what to do, and after I revealed everything to your mother, she told me to stop doubting myself and to show her daughter how I feel. So I did."

"I never knew."

"I never blatantly showed you how I felt. I didn't want you to know. I was scared, but it has never once wavered even though I wanted it to. I love you, Ruby James, more than football, more than anything else in the world. My one secret is that your mother knew how I felt as well. One day, I hope you can forgive me."

She sniffled. "What is there to forgive?" she asked. "How can I be mad at you for that?" She pushed him to the bed and straddled his waist, kissing him hard. With how she sat, she felt him harden beneath her, and she gasped at the sheer pleasure that rushed through her.

"I want you again."

"You'll get sore."

"I don't care." She gripped his neck and kissed him hard. "Theo," she said.

"What?"

"I think I'm falling in love with you as well."

In a matter of seconds, he had another condom on his hard erection, and he was at her entrance, and she slid down his length with his guidance. He showed her what he wanted, how to ride him.

She'd seen this done in the movies, but as he filled her and his hands all over her, she couldn't get enough and she didn't want him to ever stop.

Over and over, she rode his cock, feeling the pleasure begin to flood her body. One of the hands on her ass moved, and he slid his fingers between her slit, touching her clit. He stroked her to another orgasm as she rode him, and together they rode the wave to their release. She felt his cock pulse as he came, and she held onto him, not wanting to let go, feeling consumed with the need to hold him, to touch him.

Chapter Seven

The condom had broken, and now it was the countdown.

Theo didn't go and get the morning after pill. The following morning, he took Ruby home so she could talk with her dad.

He later found out that her father's name was Phil, but Theo didn't much care for the man that had broken her heart. He'd never seen her so emotional, so raw when it came to that man.

"She missed him for a long time. After school, she'd sit on the stairs for hours waiting for him to come home. It's like she couldn't imagine him not coming home. He hurt her, and even though I told him this every single time, he never turned back up."

Callie had told him this while they were making coffee.

So Phil wasn't his favorite person.

With him now back with Callie, Theo had to get used to seeing him. Ruby didn't like him being home, but she wasn't openly hostile to him anymore. She spent a lot of time with Theo when his parents were away, and he loved having her in his arms.

But still, the condom had broken, and as he stared at Ruby in the main high school corridor, he knew she was struggling not to freak out.

They'd been using condoms since, and it hadn't stopped them from being together. Having Ruby in his arms was a dream come true, only now, seeing how worried she was, he knew he had to be strong for her.

"You're sure your dates are matched up and you're not freaking out about nothing?"

"Theo, I'm late by a week. I've never been late before. It's always been like clockwork."

"Then we go and buy a test."

"If we buy a test, our parents are going to know by the end of the day. Maybe even before we know the result."

She wasn't exaggerating.

"My parents like you. Your parent likes me." This made her smile. "We can't prolong this, Ruby. We need answers." He took hold of her hand, and together they left the high school. He didn't want her worrying for the next couple of hours, and he needed to know the answer.

So, helping her into his car, he couldn't get the image of her swollen with his kid out of his head. He wasn't afraid though; he was aroused. The thought of her being pregnant filled him with joy.

He saw her hands shake as she tried to fasten the seatbelt. He took over, securing her into her seat.

"It's going to be okay."

"Is it?"

"Yes. Whatever happens, we're in this together."

He drove to the local pharmacy, and together, they picked the test that according to the packaging was the most accurate. Theo paid for it while Ruby waited in the car. One look at the cashier, who also happened to be his neighbor, and he knew he was on a countdown.

Once he was done, rushing to his car, he pulled out of the parking lot, and with speed, drove to his home.

They ran upstairs to his room, and he waited outside of the bathroom, much to his disappointment as he wanted to hold her hand as she did this.

When she was done, she opened the door, and together, they waited for the test to be ready for them to see what their future held.

"This is not bad, you know," he said.

"How can it not be bad?" she asked.

"We're together. I love you, and you adore me. We'll make good parents. Your mom is my fan. Your dad hates me though."

Ruby laughed. "I can't believe I'm eighteen years old, sneaking a pregnancy test that my mom already probably knows that I've taken."

"Yep."

"It's insane."

"Totally crazy, and insane."

"This is just so scary," she said.

He held her tightly, kissing her. Her alarm went off.

"We get to find out," he said.

They stepped toward the sink, and Theo stopped her, pulling her back against him and turning her around to face him.

"Theo, what are you doing?"

"Regardless of what that thing says, I want you to marry me."

"Theo?"

"Look, I know we're young, and people will talk regardless. I don't care. I want you to marry me. I want to be with you for now 'til eternity and beyond."

"You're going to have a bright future in football and—"

"I don't care. I don't want anything else but you. That's all I want. You're the only future I see happening. I'm asking you now, so you don't think it's because of a baby or not a baby. I want to marry you, Ruby. Even if that stick says you're not pregnant, one day, I want to have babies with you."

"You really mean this?"

"Yes. More than anything."

"Our parents could tell us no."

"Then I hope that stick says yes so we can have

what we want." He kissed her knuckles. "I mean every word I say to you, Ruby. I love you so much. I want to spend my life with you. No tricks. No nothing. Just you and me, and if you're pregnant, a little baby."

She was crying again, and he wondered if that was the hormones.

"Yes," she said.

"Yes?"

"Yes, I'll marry you." She sniffled. "We've got to see the answer."

"Okay." Not that it mattered to him. Regardless of the answer, she was going to belong to him, and he could handle anything that was sent their way, be it a baby at eighteen, or an angry dad.

Actually, he wondered how angry her father would be.

Staring down at the stick, and matching it to the results on the packaging, he saw that he was indeed going to have to face off with an angry father.

Ruby was pregnant with his baby.

He tightened his arms around her.

They both tensed as he heard the front door slam.

"Theo!"

"Ruby!"

Both of sets of parents had heard the news, and what's more, they knew they were in his bedroom.

"Do you think we can sneak out of the window and pretend we were never here?" Ruby asked.

"It sounds like a plan, but right now, I don't think we've got much choice. We've got to face them."

"I don't want to," Ruby said.

"We're engaged, Ruby. We're getting married, and now we have a baby on the way." The words were weird coming out of his mouth, but the more he thought about their situation, the happier he was. "We go down together. Also, I may have to use you as a human shield from your dad."

She chuckled. "Okay, together. We can do this. I can't believe I'm going to do this."

Holding hands, they left the safety of his bedroom, to four angry faces that were at the bottom of the stairs.

He wasn't wrong.

Phil looked ready to murder him.

****

Two months later

Ruby stared at her husband as his arms were around her. She was starting to show now, the bump of their baby pretty noticeable. Theo didn't seem to mind at all. In fact, he loved the prospect of becoming a daddy while she was freaking out. They had already come up with a plan. They were both going to college together. Theo had gotten a full scholarship, and they were even happy to help accommodate a new wife and child. In fact, they wanted to promote his sense of responsibility to the game. She'd be studying part-time, and their parents had even agreed to help out so she could still get her degree and write.

Their parents had been so angry with both of them. They had to sit side by side while for three hours straight, they yelled, argued, and told them how bad they were at making decisions.

She didn't need anyone telling her just how bad she was at making decisions, but being in Theo's arms now, as his wife, she knew she would give him everything.

"How are you holding up?" he asked.

She saw the concern in his eyes. Since they were now married, and she was nearly three months pregnant, the morning sickness kept kicking her ass, but she was coping. A lot of women handled this, and she wasn't going to be any different.

"I'm doing okay. I can't believe we're married now."

"Phil threatened to shoot me last night."

"He did?"

"Yep, he said if I wasn't here today, my life was as good as over." Theo burst out laughing. "I'm sorry. I shouldn't laugh. I love you more than anything in the world, and I think I even laughed at him."

"You didn't?"

"I totally did. I found it funny for him to think I wouldn't be here. You've been my first crush, Ruby. This, for me, is a dream come true."

"Guys are not supposed to care about their wedding."

"I'm not like normal guys. I want to be married to you. I love you, and this is the start of the rest of our lives."

"You're not afraid?"

"What do I have to be afraid of?" he asked. "I've got a beautiful wife. A child on the way. Everything. I know we're going to be the best we both can be, and, Ruby, I'll never stop loving you."

"You always say the right words."

"They're how I feel, which will always make them the right ones."

He pulled her in close, pressing his lips against hers, and she melted. He really had gotten inside her heart, and now there was no room for anyone else, just Theo.

Epilogue

Ten years later

Ruby kissed her son and watched as he walked into school. He met up with a couple of his friends, and she waited. Theo wrapped his arms around her, and she was used to several of the kids pointing in his direction.

He was, after all, a star football player.

A celebrity.

No matter his status on the field and in the sports world, he was always here for the first day and last day, for all the parent-teacher conferences, any activities that were required. His career never got in the way of being a parent, and she loved him even more for it.

"You know, this never gets easier," he said.

"Watching him go to school?"

"Watching him grow up." He kissed her neck.

Once their boy was inside school, Theo took her hand, like he did most days, and they headed back to the car. Whenever they went out a picture would always appear of them, holding hands. They were known as the football sweethearts, not that she loved football. In fact, several papers loved her dislike of the game, and it seemed to make them like her more. She didn't follow her husband around, faking it. She was straight, honest, and happy for him.

Theo helped her into the car. He stroked her thigh, and she knew she had to tell him.

She waited for them to be driving away from the school.

Having a child at eighteen had been the hardest thing she'd ever done. She didn't have the first clue how to raise a baby. With their parents' help, they both got through the long nights, the feedings, the routine, everything it meant to have a baby.

"Do you want to tell me something?" he asked, surprising her.

"Me?"

He chuckled. "Come on, Ruby. I know you, and you'd be telling me all about your latest adventure."

She wasn't published, and her stories had been rejected so many times. She didn't want the risk of being published because she was Theo West's wife, so she used her mother's name, and so far, nothing. One day, she hoped to have a book published, but Theo loved listening to her tell him her ideas.

"Also, I happen to know you're late." The car came to a stop at a red light. Theo turned to her.

"You know it's weird for husbands to know their wife's cycles, right?"

"It's not weird. Besides, I'm the one that rubs your feet, gets you ice cream, and treats you like a queen. Does this mean what I think it means?"

She saw the happiness in his eyes, and it infected her with such warmth to know he was already happy about this. "I'm pregnant."

Theo let out a whoop and pulled her in close, holding her.

"We're having another baby." He held her gently. "I've wanted another for so long, and now, are you okay?"

"Theo, baby, this is not our first baby."

"I know. He's our second. What if it's a girl? Oh my, that's it. We're going for some hot chocolate."

She burst out laughing.

Accepting his offer of a date was the best thing she ever did. As he held her hand again, locking them together, binding them, she knew there was never going to be anyone else in this world that could ever make her feel so happy.

"I love you, Theo West, so damn much."

The End

SAM CRESCENT

CRAVE HER CURVES

Curvy Women Wanted, ,14

Sam Crescent

Copyright © 2019

Chapter One

Mitch

I never in all my years thought I'd fall in love with a nineteen-year-old virgin, and yet here I am, completely, one hundred percent blown away by her sweetness. Not just how nice she is either, no—her body; damn, she's so fucking gorgeous. She didn't have the body of a teenager, but a full-grown woman. Large tits, thick, juicy, fat thighs, curves that I can't wait to get a hold of. Whenever I'm near her, all I want to do is pin her to the nearest surface and sink my cock so deep inside her. When it comes to Ava, I can't think straight. I'm the kind of guy who sees a woman, beds her, and forgets her.

Yet with Ava, I can't stop fucking thinking about her. She drives me crazy with need, and I ache for her. Watching her this past year has been torture. I haven't been able to touch her because of her father. He's nothing more than an acquaintance, but he knows how much I want her. David is a grade-A asshole. I fucking hate his guts, but what made me stay close over these three years was Ava. David saw my attraction to her. It's the only time I've ever shown any weakness. David set to exploit it. So much so, he demanded I pay for his debt. Don't worry, I paid for the debt, but now he has to deliver his daughter to me. She's not allowed to know any other details. It's all part of our agreement. He doesn't have to worry about getting broken bones, and I get Ava. If he interferes at all with my plans, the debts I've paid, I can call back in, and his ass will be in the line of fire. He doesn't care about his daughter. He's just using her, and once he's done, he'll be on his merry way, out of our lives.

Holding onto the doorframe, I watch the gravel path waiting for signs of their arrival. In a few short hours, she'll belong to me. I don't want her to know what I've done to get her, but at least her father won't get in my way.

Ava deserves someone a lot better than him. I'm determined to give her a life she deserves, one that won't be filled with worry about if food is going to be on the table. The summer at my cabin is going to be one of the best of her life. I'm not going to fail her.

The moment I see the car coming up my gravel drive, I feel my heart race. I'm not nervous. I can't wait to have her in my arms, at my mercy.

David keeps the engine running as Ava jumps out of the truck. She's wearing jeans two sizes too big and a long shirt to hide all those curves. She was bullied throughout high school. I lost count of the number of times I caught her crying because of it. Assholes. It took every single ounce of control not to hurt those motherfuckers for hurting her.

She tucks her long, blonde hair behind her ear, taking her bag from her father.

I'm not having her lift a thing. Walking down the steps, I take the bag from her, glaring at David. Doesn't he know how to be a good father? I have learned that his wife had passed away when Ava was no older than ten. Since then, he's been doing a piss-poor job of taking care of her.

Well, now it's not his concern, but mine.

"Everything she needs is there," David says. "Have fun this summer, Ava."

Without another word, he turns on his heel and leaves.

I watch him go, waiting for the car to leave before devoting my full attention to the beauty at my side. One look at her and I see her nerves kicking in.

"Have you had anything to eat?" I ask.

"No." Her stomach growls.

"Come on. Let's get you settled in and fed."

With a hand at her back, I walk up the steps, heading into the cabin.

Closing the door, I hear her gasp, and I smile. She once told me how she loved the idea of staying in a cabin for a summer, to read, relax, and not have to worry about the world around her. Well, I've granted her wish. There's nothing but the best for my woman. I'm a rich man, and I don't even have to be at my company to earn money. Just a couple of emails, telephone calls, and my business is done. I've devoted twenty years to my technology firm, and now I can reap the rewards of my hard labor.

"This is so beautiful," she says.

I've spent the past year decorating it to meet her requests. Yes, I'm obsessed with this little angel.

"I'm glad. I also purchased some paperbacks

from those authors you told me about." Taking her hand, I lead her to the small library. Again, I'm granted with another gasp. She releases my hand and rushes to the small table I've placed the books on.

"Oh my, this is … so much. My dad said you were going to help me lose weight?"

"Excuse me?"

"Yeah, he said you've agreed to help me shed this weight. I need to start taking better care of myself because I'm too fat."

I grit my teeth so hard, I'm shocked they don't snap. *Oh, baby girl, you've got no idea what I want to do to you.* Making her lose weight is the last thing on my mind.

I crave her curves. I've spent the past year working my cock with my hand just thinking about how I'm going to devote myself to exploring every inch of her.

"You're not here to lose weight, Ava."

"I'm not?" When I shake my head, she asks, "Then why am I here?"

"You're here because I want you here. I want to spend time with you, to get to know you."

"You do?"

I nod. Taking her hand and pulling her close, I rest my hand on her hip. Just from that simple touch I want so much more.

"Your father lied to you, Ava. I think you're perfect the way you are. Why don't you get settled in, and I'll fix us something to eat?"

"I'd like that."

It takes great effort to let her go. I don't want to, but there is no way I could keep hold of her just now. When I pop her cherry, she'll be spread out and ready, dripping wet before I slide my dick inside her.

I can't wait.

****

Ava

Putting my things away in my room, I'm somewhat overwhelmed by the reason for my being here. My father always had an issue with my weight, and in truth, I was tired of hearing him complain. My mother had been so slender, and seeing as I just seemed to keep on growing, it unnerved him. I don't get it though. I'm happy. I've always been happy. It's not like I eat for comfort. My size eighteen curves don't offend me.

So I've got a few extra inches. Who cares?

I mean, really, it's not like I'm going to be living with my father for much longer. Before coming here, I'd already saved up six months' worth of rent money from working my two jobs, waiting tables and working at the local library. The work isn't exactly taxing, but I like it.

With my few clothes put away, I tuck my hair behind my ears, wondering if I should get it cut or just pull it back into a ponytail.

Why would Mitch want me to spend time with him relaxing? He and my dad have been acquaintances for a while. Not too long. They met when I was about sixteen, I think. I'd just come home from school after another day of bullies, when Dad introduced us.

I'd never had a crush on anyone in my life. Why would I? All I had known most of my life is guys being dicks.

Mitch, he'd not been mean or cruel. In fact, every single time I saw him, he made me laugh.

He was my first crush, which makes this so hard. I'd not seen him for a couple of months, and during that time, I'd tried to date other men. Men who could replace my crush on my dad's friend.

Nothing worked.

I mean, seriously, what was Mitch's deal?

Why did he draw my attention so well? It's like he saw deep down into my soul, and I know that's so cliché, but come on, the guy's like a god! Well, maybe not totally like a god, but he could have any woman he ever wanted. He's been single for as long as I've known him, but in this day and age, that doesn't really mean anything.

Pulling my hair back, I tie it at the base of my neck, blowing out a breath. I really need to get myself together.

I don't know how long I'm going to be here. A few days, weeks, months? It could be anything. The drive up here, my father repeatedly told me how important it was to listen to Mitch, to do as Mitch said.

My father doesn't have the first clue about how I felt about Mitch, and what I want him to do to me. I'm nineteen years old, not dead, and certainly not immune to my sexual desires. I've never been with anyone, but ... I want sex.

When I'm around him, my body feels so achy, so wet, so ready. Like now, if I slide my fingers inside my jeans, I know I'm going to be wet.

There are times like this, I really feel I'm the wrong kind of girl. What girl fantasizes about dirty sex? The kind where her man fucks her, and makes her walk around naked, just so he could see her? I've watched a lot of porn, and rather than find it gross and disgusting, I ... yearn for it. I don't want this experience with just anyone either, but with Mitch, which is never going to happen.

Rather than hide out in my new room for however long it will be, I head back out, in time to see Mitch cutting through two large-looking sandwiches.

"Take a seat," he says, sitting at the counter.

Sliding between the counter and booth, placing my hands flat to the surface, I watch him put the sandwiches on plates.

He sits opposite me, which I don't mind. I like looking at him. Where I'm blonde, he's dark. His hair is black with a few strands of grey. He always reminds me of looking sophisticated, cute, sexy, hot. A man full of experience.

My nipples tighten to hard points.

Looking away, I grab my sandwich and take a big bite.

"So, any thoughts of college?"

With my father's mounting debts, college hasn't been in my future. I'd not been able to get a scholarship as my father refused to help me in the funding and application, much to the school's annoyance. Instead, I've worked during the past year, and while I have, I've been reapplying to a couple of colleges, hoping to finally get my spot. I doubt I'll be able to fill them, as there is now another year full of eighteen-year-olds with bright futures.

"I … I'm thinking I'll have to take courses online," I say. "I don't want to be the only girl who is a year older than everyone else. I missed my chance to go to college."

"How about we look over a few things after we've eaten? There are amazing colleges, and I'm sure we can arrange something where you can watch lectures online or something like that."

"Really?"

"Really."

He does this smile, making me wonder what he's thinking about.

"I'd love to." I really wanted to go to college. It's something I remember my mom always talking about and insisting I consider it. "The sandwich is good."

Again with the sexy smile.

I don't know how long I'm staying here, but I hope I can control my needs. The last thing I'd ever want to do is make a fool of myself. The longer I'm with him, however, the less chance I have of actually accomplishing it.

Chapter Two

Mitch

The following day, I find Ava out by the pool. I stare at her for several seconds before heading outside. She's wearing shorts with a crop shirt, and for me, it just won't do. I want her to relax and enjoy herself here, not imagine she has to constantly cover herself up. I want her to be comfortable within her own skin. This is her home as well, and I want her to be happy with being herself, and me getting to see the fruits of that.

Grabbing a couple of bottles of water from the fridge, I head out, dropping down beside her on the chaise lounge out back. She's got one of the books I purchased for her, and she places it down the moment I arrive.

"Morning," she says. "Did you sleep well?"

"I did."

"I hope you don't mind me coming out here. It just looked so beautiful, I didn't want to waste a single moment of the sun."

"You know, you should be out here in a bikini soaking up the sun. You must be way too hot in those clothes."

"No, I really shouldn't. It wouldn't be appropriate," she says.

Getting to my feet, I stare into her eyes as I lower my khakis. If I'm going to have to take the lead on this, so be it. I've got no problem with that at all. This woman is going to be mine in every single sense of the word. The sooner she realizes there's no hiding from me, the better.

With only my swimming trunks, I wink at her. "See, it's not hard."

"It's easy for you."

"Why?"

"You look … good in them."

I pause, staring at her, seeing her cheeks flame. "You're wearing a bikini right now?"

She nods her head, but I don't get any sound coming from her lips.

Taking the book from where it lies against her chest, I hold her hand, bringing her to stand up against me.

"You think you don't look good in a bikini."

"I know I'm not … really slender. Please, Mitch, don't worry about it. It's all fine."

"You're here to have some fun and relax. You're not here to lose weight. I want to see your bikini." Gripping the edge of her crop top, I pull it over her head, throwing it off to the side, out of my way. She quickly covers her chest. I don't even get a sneak peek. I'm right though. Her flesh is really warm. "I'm not going to have you passing out on me because of the heat." Going to my knee before her, I think it's very appropriate, but the ring I've got picked out for her will have to wait. She's not ready. Soon, she will be. I know she will.

Removing her shorts is not a hardship, but staring up her body, seeing her pussy covered by a small patch of fabric, is enough to drive me insane. There's no sign of her arousal either, but I know with a few touches, I'd have her soaking wet.

Standing back up, I hold her hand, and she has no choice but to stop covering up her body.

"See, I don't see a problem with the way you are. You're stunning, Ava. Beautiful. You've got nothing to hide."

She has nice, rounded thighs and stomach, and a curvy ass that I can't wait to get my hands on, to spread those sexy curves so I can see her for myself. Just looking at her is enough to make my mouth water. I'd give anything to spread her out on the chaise lounge, and take her pussy, licking her all over, and hearing her scream my name.

All in good time.

My dick is starting to harden, and I'm not exactly wearing trunks that will hide the evidence of my arousal.

"Care to join me in a swim?"

"I'd love to."

I turn my dick so she doesn't see just how hard she makes me. I've got to give her time to get used to being close to me. I have to keep repeating those words in my mind, to remind myself not to rush this kind of pleasure. It's going to be so good when I can finally sink balls deep inside her tight cunt.

The first time will be tight and she will experience pain, but after that, she's going to be thrown into such nonstop pleasure she won't be able to think.

Once we're in the pool, I release her hand and begin to swim to the opposite side of the pool, allowing her some space.

As I watch her, she slowly does a couple of laps, going through the width of the pool, before taking the length. She's a good swimmer, strong, confident. After she's done a couple of laps, she comes to my side.

"I can't believe you have a pool here," she says.

I listened to every single word she'd said about how she wanted there to be a pool to swim. She hated going to the public bathrooms, and with how she's affecting my dick, I wouldn't want her going there either.

I'm not very good at sharing what I want.

Ava's mine, plain and simple.

"You can enjoy it every time you come here."

"Thank you."

She's silent for a long time until she finally lets

go of the wall, and moves to float on her back. I watch her tits. Her thighs are pressed together so I don't get the pleasure of watching her pussy.

Get it together. She's yours now.

As per my agreement with her father, David cannot interfere or in any way manipulate Ava to his own needs. If he tries to destroy the relationship I've got with Ava, I'll call in the debt, and he'll be homeless and without any means of ever being able to have a comfortable life. In a way, he sold his daughter for comfort. I'm not going to complain.

She's mine now, and I have no intention of ever returning her.

****

Ava

Did I make a fool of myself?

I'm so nervous.

Climbing out of the pool, I go in search of a towel to attempt to dry off. My skin is so warm, and my body doesn't even feel like my own; it's like I'm someone else, not part of this life.

I want him so much, and it scares me. He's older than I am. Old enough to be my dad, but I don't see him as a dad. I see him as a man, a man I want so desperately.

When I walk back out to the pool, my book is waiting for me. Mitch is doing laps in the pool, and I can't help but watch him. I admire the sheer strength in his body as he commands the water. This is his domain, and I want him.

Pushing those thoughts aside, I take a deep breath, and quickly sit down, pressing my thighs together. There's no way I'll ever be able to have a guy like Mitch. I've heard the way some of the women from our neighborhood have spoken about him.

Even married women.

They want to bed him.

To fuck him.

To do every dirty, disgusting thing with him, and yes, I'm so jealous of them. They have a chance with him. Me? I don't.

Staring at the same page of my book for nearly ten minutes, I have to hold in my frustration. Life is so unfair. I've never been the kind of girl to have a temper tantrum, but right now, it sounds like a pretty awesome idea. Would it be so bad to scream and shout and cuss?

I don't know what to do anymore. It's so unfair, and I pout.

"Bad book?"

I nearly jump out of my skin because he's right there. His dick is so close to my face. Quickly avoiding looking at him directly, I force a smile to my lips.

"It's okay."

He chuckles. "I see the kind of books you like. Do you want me to?"

He holds up a bottle of lotion.

"What?" I'm confused.

"Do you want me to rub this on you? Your skin is going to burn really easily, and I don't want you getting in any kind of pain."

"Oh, right." Having his hands on me is going to be torture, but I can't see a reason why I should stop him. "Yes, of course."

The first touch sets me on fire. There's no other word to describe it. His hands are the best kind of feeling in the world, and I don't want him to stop. He's only at my feet, but how can someone make me feel so much from just touching my feet? It's almost criminal. Getting my thoughts together, I put the book down, dog-earing the page where I'm at. I hate doing that to books, but his hands feel so good and I forgot to pick up a bookmark.

He does each foot first, before going to my left leg and slowly sliding up to my knee. There's no way this is legal. Something this good *can't* be legal.

He does the same to the right leg, and then, he goes from my knee up. I don't think it's possible, but I'm sure for a split second, I stop breathing. His fingers are so close, like, a touch away from grazing my pussy.

Can he see how wet I am? I don't know if the bikini bottoms are the kind to show off the evidence, but for my sanity's sake, I really hope not.

Gritting my teeth, I try, I really do, to stay in control.

He moves onto the next leg, and I don't know if it's a mistake or not, but he touches my pussy. It's just his knuckles, as if he's slipped, but he does, and I can't help but gasp out. It's not pain either. This is undeniable pleasure.

I want him.

Opening my eyes, I look at him.

His dark brown eyes are so intense. It's impossible for me to look away. I don't want to. He controls me, and I can feel him everywhere.

I don't even know if it's possible to stop this. Does he know how much I want him to touch me?

I'm dying here, embarrassed. I bet he's used to more experienced women, not women who crave a man's touch so much.

Then, he does something that takes me completely by surprise. Without a single word spoken, his hand touches my pussy. It's not a mistake. This is blatant. His palm cups my pussy, and he moves up the lounge so he's close to me.

"You're wet for me, Ava."

How he says my name, the sexual roll off the tongue, there's no way I can control my need for him.

Licking my lips, I can't look away, even though I want to. I have to break this connection we have.

When he slides a finger beneath the fabric of my bikini bottoms, I'm lost. He touches me, and the slow stroke sets me on fire.

Two fingers glide through my soaking wet slit. I stare down and see his large hand, partially covered by the fabric of my bikini.

It looks dirty and yet so right at the same time. I can't stop.

"We shouldn't be doing this."

"Why not? You're old enough, and I know I am. You're wet for me. Unless you really want me to stop, why should you stop what feels so good?"

I can't think. His hand is doing really amazing things. I've never been touched by anyone else, and Mitch is making it so good.

In the next second, his hand leaves my pussy, and I can't stop the pout from forming on my lips, even though it probably makes me look like a child. I don't want him to stop.

He takes the small strings at my hips and loosens them. I lift up, and he pulls the bikini bottoms all the way from me.

This is really happening. We're really doing this.

My heart is pounding, but I don't regret this. It's like I've woken up in my dream, and now I finally get to have it.

Chapter Three

Mitch

Her pussy feels so good against my hand. I want more. I want to take her cherry so I can fuck her raw, fill her cunt with my cum and watch it flow out of her. With how wet she is, I wonder just how far I can push her. I want everything with her, and I'm so greedy, I don't think I can wait too long. With how her eyes are glazed in arousal, I know I need to take her now.

"What's stopping you? Or is it something else?"

"I don't know," she says, releasing a little whimper.

"You're so incredibly beautiful. I want to see you like this, spread open, ready to take my cock. Can I let you in on a little secret?"

"Yes."

"You're here because I want you, Ava. I've watched you this past year, and I can't wait another moment. I crave you. I've never wanted a woman the way I do you." Leaning in close, I watch her lick her lips, and I know without a doubt she feels it too.

She wants me. Craves me. Desires me.

And I'm fucking hungry for it, desperate for it. I'm in need of her in ways I've never been before.

She doesn't push me away. I can read the need for me in her eyes. I only hope she has the guts to take what I can give her.

Her nerves show, but still she doesn't push me away.

Putting my hand directly over her pussy without her bikini bottoms in the way, I watch, eagerly waiting to see what she'll do next.

"You want me to stop?" She hesitates, and as she goes to speak, I interrupt her, not wanting her to lie to me. "Only the truth. I want to hear what *you* want. Not what you think I want."

"No. I don't want you to stop."

"Good." I can't help but smile. This woman has been driving me crazy for far too long.

I want to see every inch of her. I move on the chaise lounge so that I'm straddling the chair, and she has no choice but to spread her thighs wide.

Fingering the catch at the front of her bikini top, I flick it open and watch those amazing tits spill out. She's got gorgeous breasts, with tight little nipples, and they are more than a handful. Cupping them together, I run my thumbs across each mounded peak, relishing the sound of her moan.

That's it, baby, I'm going to make every single desire you have come true.

"Please, Mitch."

The moment she says my name in that way, I nearly lose it. She's everything.

Gripping her juicy thighs, I stare into her blue eyes. Her blonde hair falls around her in waves. She looks like a beautiful mermaid, all for me.

She can be my siren.

My cock is pressed against the confines of my trunks. It's a tight fit, and I struggle to move.

"You have any idea what you do to me?" I ask.

She shakes her head.

Taking her hand, I place it over my cock. I can't wait until she gets more confident and can touch without me having to show her what I want. She's going to know my body so well.

"You're … hard?"

Standing up, I push the shorts down my thighs, kicking them off, so she can see just how hard I am for her.

Her eyes are wide, and she looks so cute, so sweet, and so innocent. I have to remember she's never been with a man before. That's okay. After today, I'm not going to wait another minute. I want her so fucking bad.

Having her outside by the pool is not going to do for me. I pick her up in my arms and smile at her squeal.

"What are you doing? Put me down. I'm too heavy."

I carry her into our cabin, and I don't get far. Sitting on the chair, I do no more than put her over my knee and spank her ass on each rounded cheek. Lifting her up, I keep her on my lap, cupping her face. "Don't you ever call yourself heavy again in my company. Do you understand me?"

"Why did you spank me?"

"You're a beautiful woman, and I love your body just the way it is. I'm not going to have you hurting yourself with your words any longer. You will listen to me. If you don't, I will punish you."

"I don't like getting hit."

"I spanked you. I didn't hit you." Sinking my fingers into her hair, I grip her head, holding her in place as I claim her lips. Finally, I get to kiss her, and it is as good as I imagined it would be. "You're mine, Ava."

Picking her up, I carry her to our bed and gently place her down on it. Last night I had to sleep alone, knowing she was only a few feet away from me, but at least she was near and I knew I didn't have to go far to get her.

Now though, she's here, in my bed. After tonight, I won't hold back. We won't share different beds. We won't be alone. I'll finally be able to show her just how much I love her and give her the life she deserves.

Kissing her plump lips, I move between her

thighs, pressing my naked body against hers. This is perfect, and exactly how I knew it would be. Actually, this is better, because she's finally in my arms, and no longer a fantasy.

Ava is real.

****

Ava

Skin to skin.

Body to body.

Feeling him against me as he kisses me, this is the thing dreams are made of. I want him so much. His arousal presses against my stomach, and I imagine him just taking me. sliding his cock in deep and I have no choice but to take it.

I should know better.

Mitch breaks from the kiss, his lips trailing down my neck, sucking on my pulse. A moan escapes my lips, and I arch up, needing him, hungry for more of him, and I know he's the only one who can give me what I need. I've never been this aroused by a book I've read.

He's not some fantasy in a book. He's real, and his lips hover just above my breasts. Keeping my eyes open, I watch him, hoping he won't call this a joke and leave. I don't think I could handle him being cruel to me.

Mitch takes one of my nipples into his mouth and sucks hard. There's immense pleasure, and as the pain seems to get a little too much, he stops and moves onto my other nipple. His tongue teases over the tight bud before he bites down.

I scream his name, arching up. I don't know if I can handle the kind of pleasure he's determined to give me.

With his lips on my tits, there's a pull deep inside me, and I know I can't let it go. I don't want to.

He presses my breasts together and groans.

"They're the best-looking tits I've ever seen. So fucking full and ripe. I can't wait to see them filled up with milk."

My heart nearly stops.

Milk.

Does he want me to have a baby?

Is that crazy?

I don't know what to say, but my body likes the idea of having his child. There's no way I would want anything else.

Mitch doesn't linger too long on my tits. His lips trail down my body, going to my hips. He presses kisses across my stomach, and I watch him as he grips my ass, holding me up.

The lips of my pussy are wet. The fine hairs glisten from how wet I am, and I know I should be embarrassed.

"Beautiful."

I cry out, flinging my head back as he swipes his tongue through my slit, teasing from my virgin entrance up to my clit. He doesn't linger on my hole. He moves up, sucking on my clit again, his teeth scoring across my nub.

The pleasure is instant, intense, and I can feel how close I am to orgasm.

All it takes is a few strokes of his tongue, and I come. Gripping the sheet beneath him, I shake, crying out his name, needing him to stop as the pleasure hits me hard and fast. I've played with myself for hours at a time during the night, to get nothing. Touching from Mitch has awakened this fire within me, and I don't know if I'm ever going to be the same again. He knows what he does to my body.

It's not my own.

I can't believe how fast my orgasm has come.

Before I can register what is happening, he's between my thighs, his hands grabbing mine as his cock presses against my entrance.

He's rock-hard. Large. Bigger than I thought possible.

When he presses against my core, I cry out.

He tears through my virginity with ease, but the pain is something I wasn't expecting. Mitch takes possession of my lips, and I can do nothing but give myself to him.

I want to throw him off and wrap my legs around him at the same time. I don't know which I want to do more, only for him to not stop.

He's everything I want, everything I need.

Slowly, achingly slowly, the pain seems to ebb. Mitch hasn't stopped kissing me, and for that, I'm thankful. I don't think I could handle him not touching and kissing me in some way. I'm hungry for him and only him.

"Please, please," I say.

"What is it you want, baby?"

"I don't know. Please, I need you." I don't even know what I'm begging for. I've read all the books. The pain has subsided and my body—he needs to move. I have to have him go harder, deeper, anything to drive the pleasure back up.

Mitch pulls out of me, and he breaks eye contact to look down at his cock. He releases a groan and drives back inside.

At first, I tense up, expecting pain, only it doesn't come.

My body is thrown into heated bliss, and there's no escape.

"Oh, baby, I knew you'd be tight, I just didn't know how much. You're all mine now. All mine, and

I'm not letting you go."

His hands let go of mine as he grabs my hips. His grip is strong, almost bruising. He pounds inside me, and rather than lie there, I begin to thrust up against him, wanting to feel him sliding in deep, wanting to feel all that he is, and to take it all.

I don't want to just experience it, I want to be part of it all, to thrust into the dirty, the kinky, and to not feel ashamed by my need for him.

Mitch has been part of my life for so long, I can't not have him there. Every time I could, I've watched him, wishing he could belong to me, and he's finally mine. I'm in his bed, he owns my virginity, and I don't want to give it to anyone else. The only person I could ever want is right here.

For me, this is a dream come true, and I don't want to lose him.

He pounds inside me, and I feel the first stirrings of orgasm, and it's so close. I don't fly over the edge though as Mitch comes, and I bask as I feel his cum fill me up, flooding my pussy.

Chapter Four

Mitch

After cleaning her up, I climb into our bed and hold her in my arms. Locking our fingers together, I get as close to her as I physically can. I want to be inside her again, but I know she needs to rest. There's only so much she can take.

Kissing her head, there are so many things I want to tell her, but I know deep down, she's not ready. This is all new for her, and I refuse to overwhelm her on the first night of the rest of our lives.

"How are you feeling?" I ask, loving how she snuggles close to me.

"Strange."

"Strange?"

"I mean, I feel … different. Is that how it's supposed to feel? Different?" She tilts her head back and smiles up at me. "I never knew it could be like this. I feel like I'm in a dream."

Kissing her lips, I slide my tongue against her mouth, and she opens up to me. She touches me with her tongue, and I growl against her lips.

"Do you have any idea what it is you do to me?"

"No."

"You make me want to not be a gentleman."

"You're being a gentleman now?" she asks.

"More than you realize." I press my face against her chest, licking the path between each tit. I want to see them bouncing in front of my face as she slides down my cock, taking me. "You see, I'm going to wait until tomorrow before I let you have my dick again."

She pouts, and it looks so cute and adorable. When I kiss her lips again, she releases a little sigh. "I could get used to this."

It's what I want.

"So, you think you can … stay?"

"Stay?"

"Where do you see yourself in five years?" I ask, distracting her.

"I don't know. I'm hoping to one day go to college, but I doubt it'll happen."

"Why?"

"I can't afford it. I'm already working two jobs just to get by. I don't think I can afford college in my future."

Oh, dear. She no longer has any job. When I agreed to the terms of the loan with David, I made sure to call her workplaces, and cancel them. I want her to myself, and I don't share. I have every intention of keeping her to myself for a lot longer than the summer.

I don't mind her going to college and pursuing her education, but everything else I want for myself.

"What if money wasn't an issue?" It never would be, but we weren't at that stage yet. One day, she will realize she will want for nothing because I give her everything her heart needs and desires.

I've been in love with her for a year. Now I've got her, and there's no way I'm letting her go.

"I'd love to be able to go to college, study English. I'd want to be a teacher, or maybe a journalist. I doubt I'd make a good teacher."

"Why?"

"I remember high school. It wasn't so long ago, and kids are so mean."

"How about kindergarten?"

"I guess. I don't know. I'd put my dreams and wishes on the back burner just in case I never got around to college." She shrugs, and I hear her wince.

"You okay?"

"Yeah, just a little sore. I'll get used to it."

Letting go of her hands, I slide them down her body, cupping her hips. They're a generous handful, and I can't wait to take her from behind.

Moving her between my thighs, I lean her back so she's resting against me.

"What are you doing?"

"I'm going to make you feel good and for you to forget about the pain." Cupping her pussy, I find her wet with a combination of our mixed release. I cleaned some of it, but there is plenty I pumped inside her.

I get my fingers nice and slick, and she gasps as I stroke over her clit.

The sound is sweet music to my ears, and as I kiss her neck, her legs spread wider, pushing her up against my hand.

That's what I want.

"I don't want you to be afraid to tell me what you want. Any dirty little thought you want, tell me."

"Mitch?"

"You're mine, and I'm yours. Whatever you want, can be yours. All you've got to do is ask for it."

She gasps even louder as I rock two fingers inside her. I don't stretch her out, getting her used to the feel of me inside her.

Drawing them back, I tease her clit, wishing I'd gotten mirrors so I could watch her. I love how she keeps arching up, thrusting her pelvis against my hand. Her tits shake with every indrawn breath.

My own cock is hard, the tip slick with pre-cum. It's impossible to *not* want her.

Her reactions are natural, sweet, and every single part of her is beautiful.

I'm going to rock her entire world, and as I listen to her come, hearing those precious sounds, I know she's going to love our time in this cabin. Bringing her down from her high, I kiss her neck just as I hear her stomach start to grumble.

"Oh, God, that is so embarrassing."

"You're hungry. It's time for me to feed my girl." Kissing her again, I move out from beneath her. "Stay here. Rest, relax. Don't do anything."

"Mitch, I'm not the only girl in the world to lose her virginity."

"No, but you're *my* girl, and I want you to relax, take it easy, and when I get back, we're going to talk about some of those fantasies of yours." I wink at her and see her face turn an even deeper shade of red.

I didn't pick those romance novels up just for her. I read them myself, and I can't help but wonder if Ava's wanting a hero all to herself.

If so, I'm more than happy to oblige.

****

Ava

The following day, I don't think I can take much more. I've had sex once, and already I'm addicted. I want Mitch again. In fact, I don't want to ever stop wanting him.

Licking my lips, I watch as he dives into the pool. His body is muscular perfection. I don't even bother trying to hide my admiration.

This man had taken my virginity, and since last night, he's treated me like a queen, which is fine.

Only … I don't want to be treated like a queen. For so long he's been the man starring in many of my fantasies. The man I imagine in place of all the heroes I read about in books. I want him. I crave him.

Does he feel the same way about me?

When we woke up this morning, I felt the evidence of his arousal pressing against my ass, but he disappeared to the bathroom.

Old nerves and insecurities have started to rear their ugly heads, and I hate myself for it. If I say anything, will he put me over his knee and spank me?

Biting my lip, I can't help but wonder what he'd do to me.

He breaks the surface at the edge of the pool, facing me, and climbs on out.

Yeah, I've got a lot of dirty thoughts. Really bad, dirty thoughts. I want him again. My pussy is so wet just thinking about all the things I've read and watched. Would it be so hard to take charge?

"I see all those dirty thoughts going on inside your head."

Tilting my head back, I cover my eyes, trying to hide from the glaring sun. It's early morning, and it is already fierce.

"What do you mean?"

In answer, he presses his hand between my thighs, and I gasp. The action is so sure, so confident, and it makes me burn even brighter.

"How about we make a deal?"

"What kind of deal?"

"You don't lie to me, and you keep these clothes off."

"You want me naked."

He tugs on my bikini bottoms, and I don't fight him as the fabric tears. Within a matter of seconds, the bikini is gone, and I'm all naked.

The smile on his lips makes it hard for me to focus on anything else.

"Spread your legs," he says, stepping back.

Opening my legs wide, I watch him, but his gaze is between my thighs.

"Touch yourself. Stroke your pussy. Let me see

you taking care of yourself."

I've played with myself many times, but with Mitch watching me, it feels a million times better, dirtier, and so right.

"Let me see your clit and your cunt. That's it. Now push two fingers inside yourself. Oh, baby, that's fucking perfect. So sexy. Keep on pushing inside. Again, do it again."

It is hard to keep my eyes open as he is determined to make me lose my mind. He pushes down his boxer briefs and starts to stroke himself, going from the base of his cock up to the tip and back down again, drawing back his foreskin to reveal the bulbous tip.

Pre-cum coats his cock, and I want to taste him.

I've watched a lot of women sucking on cock, and seeing how magnificent he looks, like an Adonis or something like that, I want to be at his mercy.

"Tell me what you want."

How does he do that?

"I want to taste you." My mouth is so dry, and he smiles, stepping forward.

"Good, because I can think of nothing better than having those pretty lips wrapped around my dick."

He presses the tip to my lips, and I open up. Without warning, he slides inside, and I stare up the length of his body as he hits the back of my throat. For a split second, I worry, but he doesn't give me a chance to panic as he pulls out. The tip slides across my lips, leaving a drop of his pearly white pre-cum.

I lick it up, and he goes back into my mouth.

I close my eyes, but Mitch has other ideas. He grips my hair, wrapping it around his fist, holding me in place. If I was to pull away, it would hurt.

My nipples are so incredibly tight and my core aching. I feel like a slut, a wanton, dirty slut, and there's nothing else I want more than to have him, than to be with him.

"Don't use your teeth. I don't want you biting it off."

Heat fills my cheeks, but I make sure my teeth are nowhere near his length. This time as he slides into my mouth, only my lips touch him as I suck, hard. Saliva fills my mouth, and I try to swallow it down, only some dribbles out. His dick is completely coated as he begins to pump into my mouth. I don't wipe the saliva from my chin. I hold his cock, working his length as I saw those women do, wanting to feel his cum fill my mouth.

I'm terrified, excited, exhilarated, and desperate for more.

He doesn't stop until I take as much of him as I can. When he's close, he tells me to be ready.

"Don't swallow. I want to see it in your mouth."

His words make me even wetter. I love his groan, and I wait as he fills my mouth with wave upon wave of his cum until it's almost overflowing.

Once he's done, he stares down at my face, cupping my cheek.

"Now swallow."

Closing my lips, I do as he says.

"Let me see."

Opening my lips, I wait for him.

"Good girl."

I cry out as he slams his lips down on mine, and kisses me. He grips my ass and surprises me again as he lifts me up in his arms. I'll never get bored of the way he holds me. I feel like a princess in his arms.

He doesn't stop kissing me, not even when we get to the bed, or as he slides inside me. There's a bit of pain, but nothing I can't handle.

Chapter Five

Mitch

Ava ran away from me, through the forest where a lot of tourists used to hike. We'd needed a break from the cabin because the four walls were driving me crazy, but also, I wanted to show Ava I wasn't ashamed of being seen out with her. We had gotten to talking about our life back home, and she seemed to be under this impression we were going to remain a secret.

Fuck that shit.

There's no way I'm keeping my feelings about her a secret. I love her, and I intend to get a ring on her finger, stat. I'm not a fool and I know someone will see what a precious gem she really is, and when that happens, I'm not going to be the one to lose her.

I catch up to her, and wrap my arms around her waist. She's laughing so hard as she leans forward, trying to get away from me.

When I spin her around, she starts to giggle. I've not heard the sound enough.

Pressing her up against the tree, I capture her hands, placing them above her head and hearing her moan just as I kiss her.

Her body melts at my touch. When I thrust my cock against her, she lifts her leg up and begins to rub herself against me. It feels so good that I start to wonder why I even left our cabin.

Ava breaks the kiss first, ducking down and running off.

I let her go. I've already caught her, and there's no chance of her ever letting go of me.

Watching her run, I give her a few seconds to think she can get away from me, until I can't handle it anymore.

We pass some walkers, and I give them a nod before rushing past them. They don't need to know my business.

This time, when I catch her, I lift her off her feet, forcing her to wrap her legs around my waist. She holds the back of my neck, and I move off the path so no one can see us, circling a tree to shield us.

"You're being naughty," she says.

"I know what I'm doing."

"What if we get bitten by a bear?"

"Then we were really unlucky." I bite at her lips, letting out a growl.

She laughs, and as she does, her pelvis rubs against my dick. "I need you. Let's go back to the cabin, please."

I love hearing her beg.

"I'm not moving from this spot."

"But I want you."

"You want my dick?" I ask. I love seeing the glint in her eye, the sparkle I've never seen her have with anyone else. This is exclusive to me, and I intend to keep it, to nurture it.

"Yes."

"Then we don't need to go to the cabin for you to enjoy that."

Her teeth sink into her lip, and she lets out a little gasp.

"You can have it right here." Keeping her pressed to the tree, I place one hand above her head, and with the other, I grip her ass. "You want it?"

"But people could hear."

"Only if you don't be quiet. What do you say, dirty girl? You want a little adventure?"

"Yes."

"Then take out my dick. I'll give you what you

need."

She reached between us, loosening my jeans and taking out my cock. I'm so hard, and she scores my length against the pinch of the zipper. Letting out a hiss, I muffle the sound against her neck. Her actions are still so inexperienced. Where some men might be pissed, I love it. She's all mine, and I'll teach her everything she needs to know.

"You better not be wearing any panties."

"I'm not."

I went through her suitcases and threw them all in the trash. I have a couple of pairs stored away for that time of the month. If I get my way, however, I want her knocked up. I wanted her bound to me in every single way that counts.

Kid.

Marriage.

Mine.

Plain and simple.

To some, I'm an asshole for doing this, but I'm the best man for Ava. I know what she needs. I've seen people hurt her one too many times, and I couldn't do anything about it. This time, I'm going to do everything in my power for her to be happy.

I tug her skirt up so there's nothing between us.

"Put me inside you."

She places my cock at her entrance. Her hand shakes a little, and I wait, patiently. Pre-cum is already leaking out of the tip.

When I'm an inch inside her, I slam forward and press my palm against her mouth to contain the scream as I fill her tight cunt.

Licking her pulse against her neck, I slowly rock in and out of her, taking more of her. In the distance I hear the sound of walking groups.

Ava's eyes go wide, but I don't stop. I keep on fucking her.

"Touch yourself," I whisper to her.

She shakes her head, and my grip on her ass tightens so she has no choice but to do as I ask.

She gives in, moving those fingers against her clit, and I feel her pussy tighten around my length.

Pulling out, I slide back inside. Over and over, I fuck her, making her have all of me even as people pass us. I don't stop. She's so close. The flutters of her pussy nearly send me over the edge, but I don't give in. I wait.

Only when she finds release, and the sounds of her orgasm are muffled by my hand, do I find mine. When I do, I fill her pussy and can't stop. The pleasure is so intense, and I need more of her.

I'm hungry for her.

One lifetime will never be enough. Not for me. Not when it comes to Ava.

****

Ava

I've lost track of how long I've been here. Sitting on the sofa, I watch Mitch in the kitchen. He's making us up a stir-fry, and my thoughts are all a mess. We've been here forever, and yet, I don't want to leave.

What if leaving here, I have to go back home? Back to my mundane life of always wondering what it would be like with him. Now, I know, and can I go back to pretending not to want it? I love every waking and sleeping moment. From the moment I open my eyes and feel him surround me, I feel safe, happy, contented. I don't want to be with anyone else.

He is all I want.

All I need.

"Good book?" he asks.

"I'm not really reading it." I've not done a whole

lot of reading since I arrived here. I love this cabin. I love my time with Mitch.

I love … Mitch.

It's not a big shock to me. I knew he meant something to me long before this revelation. I just didn't realize how much.

"What's wrong?" he asks, moving around the kitchen counter to capture my face before giving me a kiss.

What *is* wrong with me? I'm scared of losing him?

I don't want to be alone, and I know if we leave here, there's a risk of that. It's so strong, I can feel my heart breaking. It's so acute, so sharp, so everything.

Mitch smells like peppers and onions.

"Shoot, I don't want to burn the food."

He kisses the top of my head before walking away. I watch him as he finishes splashing in some soy sauce and a little honey before working the noodles and vegetables together by tossing the ingredients. He looks very chef-y as he does this. He serves us both up in two bowls, with chopsticks to eat with.

We don't sit at the kitchen counter but take our food into the sitting room. Staring across the room, I'm very much aware of him beside me.

Out of the corner of my eye, I see his legs. It's not a big thing, but they remind me of how he feels as he slides inside me, his thighs keeping mine spread open, taking him. The memory brings an instant pool of heat in my groin.

"So, when we head back home, I wanted to know if you'd like to live in my country home or my penthouse apartment, or back in our old neighborhood?"

"You have a country home and a penthouse apartment as well?" I'm shocked.

Mitch chuckles. "I think I forgot to tell you. I'm wealthy. Worth a couple of million. We can move around and live wherever you want."

I take a bite of my chicken, feeling a little nervous.

He's rich?

"Erm, I don't know."

"Well, as much as I'd like to stay here forever, I want to put your touch on my other places. I think you'll like them."

Does this mean he wants me to be part of his life?

My heart skips a beat. Mitch is always surprising me.

"I … I'm a little confused right now."

He doesn't speak, simply takes the bowl of food from my hands and places both bowls on the coffee table.

My heart is pounding. I'm so scared and panicked and also a little excited, especially when he goes on one knee.

"Ava, I don't want our time to come to an end in this cabin. I also don't want you to think I'm hiding you away as some kind of secret. Far from it." He reaches out, stroking some hair behind my ear.

Biting my lip, I watch him, hungry for more of his touch. For more of him. I don't want him to stop, so when he takes my lips, I cup his face, kissing him back.

"Ava, I want you to come and live with me. To be part of my life and I want to give you the world. College, whatever else your heart desires. I'll cook for you as well."

It's not an admission of love, but it is something, and I can handle all the rest. Pressing my lips against his, I kiss him hard, sliding my tongue across his mouth how he's showed me. During my time here, Mitch has shown me a great deal, from how to kiss, to exploring his body.

He draws me down onto the rug beside the fireplace. It's too hot to have a fire, but one day we may do it in the colder months. Mitch strips out of his clothes, and I help him by ridding my body of my own until we're both completely naked.

This is different. He kisses his way down my body, lavishing attention on each breast before moving between my spread legs. His cock finds my entrance and slides in deep. He doesn't go fast.

Locking our fingers together, he takes his time, slowly, inch by inch, working his length within me, making sure I can take all of him before he pulls out, and then proceeds to slide back inside me.

Each time, he goes deeper and deeper. His cock is branding me, but I have never felt closer to him than I do in this very second.

It's consuming.

It's needy.

It's everything I've ever wanted.

When he growls my name against my flesh, it makes me feel so alive, so loved. It's everything I've ever wanted, and he continues to give. Before he finds his own release, he makes sure I find mine, coming all over his length before he picks up speed, working himself inside me, until I feel the pulse and spill of his cum.

This isn't cold, hard fucking.

Mitch has just made love to me.

It is the first time we've done it so passionately, and now I don't know if he loves me, or if he's just showing me what he wants.

Chapter Six

Mitch

Ava hates the penthouse apartment, but she's making it work, especially because on the rarest of the rare occasions, I've had to go into my office. Now that we've come away from the cabin, and she actually gets to see my life, she's a little … perplexed.

She tries to hide it in her sweet smiles, but when she thinks no one is looking, I see the fear in her eyes. She doesn't know what to do. If she thinks for a single moment I'm not looking or paying attention to her, she is so wrong.

I've wanted this woman for so long, and the month we've spent at the cabin is just the start of forever. Ava still thinks she's going back to her father, as I've not told her yet that I'm never giving her back.

My only wish right now is to tell her the truth of how I feel.

I'm getting tired of her worrying for no good reason.

Like right now, I know there are a couple of receptionists in my building who want to fuck me and find any excuse to see me in person. Each time they arrive, Ava gets even quieter and seems to sink down even more into the sofa. She's not reading one of her favorite authors though, no, she's spending her time reading several different college applications. There are so many places she can choose from.

Once the receptionist, whose name I don't remember, leaves, I look toward the woman I do love.

She's staring at the door.

Pressing the intercom, I tell my PA to hold all visitors and not to disturb me until I say otherwise.

"Ava, come here," I say.

She's a little startled when I say her name.

Closing her booklet, she puts it down on the sofa and walks toward me. I've purchased her many different items of clothing, and this blue dress has a nice, flowing skirt, which if she was to spin around would flow out and showcase her thighs. I hold my hand out for her to take, which she does, and I pull her toward me, making her straddle my lap. Pressing my cock against her pussy, I feel her moan, and watch her eyes close as I rub against her sensitive area.

She's been with me a month and a half, and I know she has already skipped a period, but I wonder if she has even realized it yet. I want to know if she's carrying my child so I can take the next step of owning her and showing her for the rest of our lives, just how much I love her.

Gripping her ass, I rub her against me, loving how her eyes close and her head tilts back as I hit the right spot, the spot I know she loves.

She doesn't hold back as I give her what I want. My dick hardens even more.

She straightens up, her hands going to my shoulders.

"You want me?" I ask.

"Yes."

"Beg me for it."

"Please, Mitch, I want you. I need you. Please. I'll do anything. Please."

I love it when I get her like this, when her need overrides everything else. It's hypnotic, and what makes it even better is she's all fucking mine.

I don't share. I hate sharing, and with Ava, I can be as selfish as I need to be.

Lifting up her skirt, I trace my finger across the seam of her panties. They're wet from her arousal, and it makes me even harder to know my girl can be just as dirty as I am.

"Take out my cock."

She lowers the zipper of my pants, her hand sliding in to touch me.

I'm so hard and already slick with my pre-cum. I grip the edge of her panties and yank hard, feeling them tear, and I shove them into my pocket. Holding her hips, I lift her up, and she grasps my cock.

We work together, and as I sink inside her, we both moan our pleasure.

Even though I've been fucking her for a month straight, she's still too tight. Each time I fuck her, it's like a vise is wrapped around my dick, and there's no way of stopping it. I love how tight she is, and I want her. I want her so fucking much.

Every waking moment is filled with my need for her, and it doesn't stop, not even for a moment. I want to give her the world. I'm obsessed with her, and there's no mistaking my feelings for her.

She means everything to me.

My entire world is surrounded by her.

I love her.

I want to claim and own every part of her.

When I think she is pregnant with my child, I can't help but feel … happy, thrilled, excited. I want to go and get a test, but I also don't want to freak her out.

I love her more than anything else in the world. There's no one I want more, and I can see us having a life together.

A happy, fun-filled life.

Gripping her hips tighter, I rock into her, going as deep as I can, lifting her up and pulling her back down onto my cock. Over and over, I fuck her, going deeper inside her, watching her eyes as they dilate.

The pleasure is building between the two of us.

I don't want to come without her.

Moving her skirt out of the way, I finger her pussy, working her over and over until I feel the flutters of her cunt as she comes over my cock. With the tightness of her pussy, and the feel of her cum, I fill her up again, hoping my seed has already filled her, wanting to keep her as mine, and not let anyone else touch her.

She belongs to me.

Only to me.

Sinking my fingers into her hair, I pull her close, and slam her lips against mine, nipping at her flesh.

She is mine.

****

Ava

When I walk around his country home, I feel like this is where I'm meant to be. The end of summer is fast closing in, and I'm worried about what waits for me when I go home. I've got no job for me, and I love being here. I love being with him. Mitch has gone out to run some errands, and promised to return soon as he wanted to talk. Biting my lip, I stare into one of the spare bedrooms. His country home has over six rooms, three of which have always been designed for guests. This one is different though. As I stare into the room, I can see it changing, becoming a nursery, and without thinking, my hand goes to my stomach. More than anything I want to have this baby.

Mitch doesn't know. When he was in a meeting the other day, I snuck out of the building to the pharmacy and purchased a test. I took it in the bathroom, and I wasn't surprised when the blue lines confirmed I was indeed pregnant. I wonder how Mitch will feel knowing we've made a child together.

I've never felt so terrified in my life.

I'm in love with a man who hasn't even said how he feels about me.

I know he desires me, but can that ever go to love? Can it ever be more?

I doubt it.

I hate being a pessimist. All my life I've only known sadness and betrayal until Mitch. He's the only man who has ever given me hope.

I could see a small crib in the center of the room with an animal dial hanging down and a nightlight casting stars around the darkened room.

Each thought makes me yearn for more.

I've known Mitch for a couple of years, and he's been my lover now for several weeks. I can't imagine my life with anyone else, but what if he doesn't want to be with me?

When his arms wrap around my waist and his lips brush my neck, I close my eyes.

"Should I be worried you're staring into an empty room?" he asks.

"No."

"I've made reservations for tonight. It's the French place you love so much."

"Yes, you want to talk, right?"

"Yes."

He kisses my neck again. "Come on, baby. Let's go and get ready."

I follow him out of the room, taking the cowardly way out.

Tucking my hair behind my ear, I cut off my self-doubts and focus on the man in front of me. The way he takes charge. Showering together is a dream come true with how he devotes so much time to caressing my body. Each touch, caress, and stroke only serve to enhance my need for him.

Tonight is different though. Mitch doesn't press me up against the tiled walls and fuck me. He turns the water off, and I'm shocked.

I follow him out of the shower and dry myself off before going into our shared closet. All the new clothes I own were picked out by Mitch. I don't mind. He's got exquisite taste in clothes.

Running my fingers over the fabric, I pick out the perfect red dress. It's the kind that molds against every single curve of my body. I won't be able to wear this soon as my pregnancy starts to show.

Once I'm done, I turn to Mitch, and his gaze travels down the length of my body. There's no mistaking the heat in his gaze. It lingers on my hips, and I wonder if he can see the evidence of what we've made together.

It takes every single ounce of control not to touch my stomach, but I do it.

"You look stunning."

"Thank you."

Holding his hand, we make our way down to his car. He opens the door for me, always the perfect gentleman. I can never complain about his treatment of me because he always makes me feel cared for and loved.

On the way to the restaurant, he turns on the radio, and I can't help but feel nervous. We usually talk about our days, and he tells me about how annoying he found his latest meeting. I like how he shares his life with me, but now, something is different, and I wish we could go back.

There's no going back though.

No matter how much I want it.

We can't change what we've done.

I fist my hand at my side, stopping myself from

touching my stomach. All in good time. I've got to be patient and wait.

I'll tell him later tonight, after he's talked about whatever it is he wishes to discuss. I hate that I'm taking the cowardly way out, but my nerves are shot.

Arriving at the restaurant, Mitch gets out of the car and stops the valet from helping me. He still doesn't like the idea of any other man touching me.

I find it so sweet. It gives me hope.

With his hand at my back, we walk into the restaurant. Aware of the stairs, I hold onto Mitch's arm as the maître d' shows us to our table.

Mitch only gets the best. He told me how he built his company from the ground up, learning from his past mistakes, to become the man he is now. He doesn't have to spend every waking moment at work, but there are rare occasions he's called in to handle certain matters. I don't mind. I happen to enjoy watching him work. He's a commanding presence in any domain he enters.

My love for him hasn't wavered, not once.

"We'll have a glass of wine," Mitch says.

"Can I just have water? I'm not in a drinking mood." I need to see a doctor to go through all of the pregnancy dos and don'ts. I'm so far out of my depth, but Mitch nods toward the waiter.

"Water?"

"I hope that's okay. Unless this is a celebration?" I can fake drink the wine until I tell him the truth.

"It's fine. Water, pop, wine, drink whatever you want."

Is this so he can break up with me? I hate how my heart seems to break. Tears fill my eyes, and I quickly look down so he doesn't see.

Chapter Seven

Mitch

I can't stand to see her cry, and the moment she bowed her head, I knew she was trying to ward off tears.

Reaching across the table, I hold her hands and will her to look at me.

When that doesn't work, I beg her to.

"Baby, look at me. Don't do this. I want to see your pretty eyes." So far tonight, it's not going well. First, I screw up by being late home. Then I catch her staring at the spare bedroom with no furniture, and I worry she wants to leave me. Then, because I'm late, I can't take my time in the shower with her.

My dick is in desperate need to be inside her, and instead of enjoying the fun, I'm stuck having to rush her along.

Then to make matters worse, her dress molds to every curve, which only serves to scream at me for making these stupid reservations. I could cook for us or order out. Only, I wanted this to perfect.

I should have known anything perfect for us, would be with just the two of us.

"Don't cry."

"It's nothing."

"You look like you're going to cry. That's not nothing. It's something."

"I've got something to tell you, and I'm afraid."

My heart trips over. I can't believe how quickly this woman unravels me.

"Tell me after I ask you something," I say. I need to do this now, as otherwise I'll lose my nerve.

Keeping hold of one of her hands, I reach into my pocket and grab the ring.

"Ava, I love you. I know I've not told you, but I

"Yes. I don't know what I'm doing."

Gripping the back of her neck, I pull her close, kissing her lips. "We're going to be doing this together, that's what. You, me, and our child."

Kissing her again, I once again wish we were at home, only we're surrounded by people.

I sit opposite her as the waiter comes to take our orders. I let Ava order first before giving him my own. I don't care about the food.

"You've not answered my question," I say. I've still got the ring, and she gasps.

"Yes. I want to marry you. I want to be your wife."

I slide the ring onto her finger, and I'm not surprised to find it fits perfectly. Exactly how I knew it would.

There is no backing out now.

She is my wife.

Around the restaurant there are rounds of applause, and I bask in them as I lean over the table to cup my fiancée's face. She kisses me back with an equal passion, and my dick hardens. I don't even care where we are anymore. There's only one woman for me, and it will always be her.

The waiter brings us out our food, and I hold Ava's hand as I eat. It's awkward, but right now, knowing she's pregnant, I don't want to let her go, not for a single second.

"You wanted to propose? That's what you wanted to talk to me about?" she asks.

"Yes. I wanted it to be the perfect setting even though now, I feel our bedroom would have been the perfect place."

She chuckles. "You're having to be on your best behavior."

do. The truth is, I paid off your father's debts to make sure he didn't interfere with us. I want you all to myself, and I have for some time now. I know you're only nineteen, but there's no one else I could ever want. I'll give you everything, if you just say yes."

The tears that were in her eyes start to fall, and I feel like the biggest fucking loser around.

"What?"

"I want you to marry me, Ava. I want you to be my wife." I'm aware of people staring at us, but I couldn't give two shits. The only person I care about is the woman staring at me in shock. "I kind of need you to speak."

"I'm pregnant."

Okay, I wasn't expecting that. "You are?"

She nods, sniffles, and glances around the room to see we're being watched.

"Hey, hey, ignore them. We have every right to be here as well." I hold her hand a little tighter. She only needs to focus on me. "I love you. I want to marry you."

"But I'm pregnant."

"Look at me, I don't mind. I think that's fucking brilliant." I pick her hand up and kiss her knuckles. "I want to have a family with you. I want to have it all with you. Every single moment of my life I want it to be with you, not with anyone else." Getting up from my chair, I crouch down beside her, wiping away her tears. I can't bear to see my baby cry. "I love you more than anything else in the world."

"You do?"

Placing my hand over her stomach, I smile. "Yes. We're going to have a baby?"

"Yes, I took a test. We're going to have a son or daughter. I don't know which."

"That's why you didn't want the wine?"

"Yes. Can I ask you a question?" I ask.

She nods.

"Are you angry with me about your dad?"

"No. My dad and I have never really seen eye to eye. I can imagine he was more than happy to get rid of me." She squeezes my hand. "I'm sorry if he caused you any trouble."

"He means nothing to me. I stuck around for you. You needed someone, and he proved time and again, he wasn't worth my time."

We finish our meal and forgo dessert. I get the check, and with her hand in mine, I lead her back out to the car.

Home is the only place I want to be.

For now until eternity.

****

I giggle as Mitch turns the instructions over again and again. We had our pregnancy confirmed today at the doctor. It is too soon to tell the sex, but seeing as we now have a baby on the way, he is going crazy over getting the nursery set up.

He loves the same room as I do. It's close to our bedroom and has the perfect view of the garden.

Resting my head against the doorframe, I place a hand on my stomach.

"Are you reading the instructions right?" We're going to get married this weekend. I don't want a large wedding, and neither does Mitch. We're flying out to Vegas to make it official. Some women want huge church weddings. Me, I just want to marry him. I don't need anything else attached to it, just Mitch.

He looks up at me, and the glare disappears.

"They've sent the wrong instructions with the crib." He gets to his feet and walks toward me, showing me his manly skills are not to be questioned. I smile.

"I see."

"You should be resting."

"I know a whole lot of other women who were heavily pregnant and still working. I'm not even out of my first trimester yet. I'm good." Stepping into the bedroom, I look at all the pieces. "How about we work on this together?" I grab his phone, bringing up the crib and the description of how to put it together.

For the next two hours, with a lot of laughter and some tickling, we were able to put it together. Once it is done, we stand back, admiring our handiwork. We've done it, built a crib together, but I know just from looking at it we've done so much more than that.

"How are you feeling?" he asks. His hands are on my stomach as I stand in front of him. He worries about everything and nothing.

"I'm fine."

"You don't need to go and rest?"

"I don't need to go and rest." Spinning in his arms, I ask. "Do you want a sandwich?" I cup his cheek and smile up at him.

"Are you happy?"

This makes me pause. "You think I might be … unhappy?"

I love it when he holds my face. It's always so gentle and with the slight edge of dominance I can't resist. "I want you to be happy."

"Mitch, I've never told you this, but … erm … I've been in love with you since I was sixteen. Whenever you'd come around, I'd hide because I was afraid you'd see it. My feelings for you have only gotten deeper. Then when I turned eighteen, I knew I was in love with you. When I read the romance books, I'm not reading them for the hero. I was always imagining you in those roles." Placing my hands on his chest, I look up into his face and offer him a smile. "You're my everything, and you have been for a long time. Happy doesn't even begin to cover what I am. You make me complete."

"Yep, you're not getting a sandwich for a couple of hours." Mitch lifts me up over his shoulder and carries me out of the room down to our bedroom.

I can't wait.

Since finding out about the baby, he'd been so careful with me, whereas now, he knows he doesn't have to be.

We can have sex and fun for some months to come.

I, for one, can't get enough of my soon-to-be husband, and I love that he can't keep his hands off me.

Epilogue

One year later

Standing at the edge of the pool at our cabin, I watch my wife hold our daughter in her arms. Ava gave birth to her three months ago, and we felt it was only time for us to get away from the city.

The cabin has been calling to us for some time. This is where we kick back, have fun, and just enjoy each other. I get off the phone from work, and now I climb into the pool and walk over to my two darling girls. Ava is glowing as she always does, and so is Bethany, our baby girl.

Both of them gave me a fright on the day Bethany was born. Hearing Ava in pain during the birth, I honestly wasn't prepared for any of that, and then, my daughter's first cry as she came into this world.

I loved my daughter instantly as the doctors placed her on my wife's chest.

Cupping the back of Bethany's head, I hold her in my arms, and Ava snuggles against me.

"I know you want to wait, but don't you want to fill our very large house with more of these?" she asks.

"I do. More than anything."

"Then why are you so determined to wait?"

Staring into her blue eyes, I kiss her lips. "I've got my reasons."

"Let me hear them."

Looking down at Bethany, I sigh. "Shall I tell Mommy all the reasons I want to wait to have a baby?" Bethany doesn't say a word, but her cuteness is a massive overload. "Because I don't want to share her with anyone else. I can't stand to hear her cry out in pain, and above all else, I don't think I can go through the risk of anything happening to you." I lift my head up and look into her eyes. "I love you, Ava. I can't imagine my world without you in it, and I refuse to settle."

She wraps her arms around my neck, pulling my head down to her lips. "I love you, Mitch. I can wait for more kids. I've got you and Bethany."

And she's completing her college education online, but I don't bring that up. I know deep down, she's actually loving being a mother.

With my wife in one arm, my baby girl in another, I can't help but think of Ava heavily pregnant with my child. Just watching her turned me on. The sex was incredible. It's still amazing now, but she had pregnancy hormones.

Maybe I won't make her wait too long.

After all, I'm still a selfish bastard at heart when it comes to Ava. I always want more.

The End

SAM CRESCENT

THE MAFIA'S CURVY WOMAN

Curvy Women Wanted, 15

Sam Crescent

Copyright © 2019

Prologue

There was something sexy about watching a woman take care of children. Marco Guidi stared across the garden of the man he was currently visiting to do business with. Dean Marshall helped the mafia out whenever they needed him, and in return he got to live a life of total luxury with his wife and kids.

One of those kids was none other than twenty-one-year-old Petal, who had his attention and had been holding it since she turned eighteen. He shouldn't keep coming here. It would get suspicious, but when it came to Petal, Marco had no control over who he wanted.

She was the reason he made every excuse he could to see Dean.

The man was good at what he did, clearing computers and creating new identities as well as making people disappear.

"This is everything you need," Dean said, handing him a large brown envelope.

"Thanks." Marco grabbed the envelope, taking a peek inside just to make sure. Dean was good, but if at any point he thought he could get away with shitting on them, Marco had no qualms about putting a bullet in his head.

"It's all there. You know I'm good for it." Dean rubbed his hands on his jeans.

"I've got to check." Once he was satisfied, he pulled out his much smaller envelope with the money needed to pay, but held it back as he looked toward Petal.

"Why don't we trade something else?" Marco asked.

"Excuse me?" Dean looked from Marco toward where Petal was standing and back again. "Oh, I know why you come here, Marco."

"Mr. Guidi." He reminded the other man of his place.

"Sorry, Mr. Guidi. Petal is a beautiful girl."

"I know. So why don't you tell me about her?"

"You want to know if she's a virgin? Yes, she is. She's sweet and kind too. No guy has been sniffing around her."

He liked that. "I want her."

"She's twenty-one."

"I don't care about her age."

Dean looked toward his daughter as if he wanted to disagree.

"I will only ever conduct business with you. I will also raise my other payments by twenty percent for each request I make of you." Marco knew he was making the man an offer he couldn't refuse. "I'll take care of her, and she'll want for nothing."

"You want to give me money and take my daughter as well?"

"Yes. Do we have a problem?" Marco could take her if he wanted. He didn't need to make a deal like this. Whatever he wanted, he got.

Marco wasn't normally the kind of guy to take human beings as payment. This was a personal transaction between him and Dean. He needed information on one of the Capos who he believed was taking bribes from the local cops, but he also wanted Petal, and he'd been wanting her for some time now.

Normally it was the cops in their pocket, but it would appear this Capo had been put in a vulnerable position and now it was up to Marco to deal with it.

One more glance over at Petal, he couldn't deny how captivating she was. There was only so much he could take, and he'd denied himself so many times. Would it really be wrong to take her for his own? No, he didn't think it was.

"Not many guys would take her. She's too fat for them."

Marco wanted nothing more than to grab his gun and shoot the bastard's fucking face off. Petal wasn't a slim girl. She had curves, and they were in all the right places. Nice, full tits, more than a generous handful. Her waist was small, but flared out into wide hips that made him want to hold her as he fucked her hard. Her thighs were not small either. She didn't have the gap between, but he wanted them wrapped around his waist as he pounded inside her.

He wanted this curvy woman all to himself.

"Deal?" pressed Marco.

"Deal," Dean said.

He was more than willing to take Petal off of Dean's hands. What the other man needed to realize was he wasn't going to get his daughter back.

Chapter One

Petal wasn't stupid. Her father and mother liked to pretend she didn't have a brain or that she couldn't hear. They wanted to keep her wrapped up in a tight little bubble where she didn't know they worked for the mafia or did a lot of illegal shit. She knew they were on the local law enforcement's watch list.

She had seen them come in and arrest her father in the middle of the night. By the time morning came, her father was back home and not a mention to him being escorted out of the house at night.

Just like she knew arriving at Marco Guidi's apartment in the middle of the city wasn't some housekeeping job. She had heard her parents talking. They didn't like having her around the house. She asked too many questions, and they were worried she'd open her mouth or talk to the wrong kind of person.

She loved her family very much, though maybe a little less as she knew she was being sold. She'd never, ever snitch on her family. They meant the world to her.

Still, she stood in the middle of the sitting room, waiting.

Marco Guidi.

He was a handsome man. Sexy in a dark, mysterious kind of way. Whenever she looked at him, his gaze always seemed to hold dark secrets.

Secrets she knew she shouldn't want to know but intrigued her still.

There was no denying an attraction to him, and knowing she'd been "sold" to him turned her on. She wasn't ignorant of the kind of man he was either.

Maybe she should be.

Marco confused her in every single way.

He was a deadly man, fierce, strong, and she had

no doubt he'd killed a lot of people in his time.

Still, her want of him hadn't diminished or faded, even knowing partially what he was capable of.

Running her fingers through her brown hair, she looked around the pristine apartment.

There was no reason for him to have a housemaid. From how clean the apartment was, she figured he had someone he trusted come in a couple of times a week.

Stepping over to the windows, she quickly moved back.

Heights were not her thing. She was terrified of them, and even when she watched movies based on heights, her body got all sweaty.

"It's a wonderful view," Marco said.

She spun around to see the very man himself in the main living room, watching her. She hadn't even heard him come in.

"Were you here?" she asked.

"No, I stepped out."

"Oh."

"Do you like the view?"

"It's lovely."

He wore one of his classic suits. She had noticed her only ever wore black suits, and once again, he was in black. Did he always expect to attend a funeral?

"You're afraid of heights?"

She glanced behind her, not wanting to look down. "A little bit, yeah."

"I'm afraid it's something you're going to have to get used to."

"I guess." She pressed her hands together, not really sure what she should or shouldn't be doing. "What kind of job is it that I've got?"

"Your father told you it was a job?"

"Yes." She nodded her head.

Marco walked closer to her. Each step he took, Petal found her body responding to him. She wanted him to touch her, to put those huge hands on her and make all of her fantasies come true.

Living with her father, she'd been restricted in everything she could do. She wasn't allowed to attend a regular high school. She'd been shipped off to an all girls' school, only allowed to return when he wanted her around or for the holidays.

The men around her always kept their distance, until now.

Marco was the first man she had been alone in a room with. Her father or mother would always miraculously enter a room.

She often wondered what it would be like without her meddling parents, but she had yet to find out.

Petal had no choice but to tilt her head back as Marco advanced closer to her.

"I don't want you cleaning my place, or touching anything."

"Then why am I here?" she asked.

His lips were so close.

She'd never been kissed. Never even been felt up by a guy.

The only thing her father hadn't restricted was her reading. She could read as much as she wanted for as long as she wanted. She had absorbed every kind of romance there was, and even more so. Anything that was related to romance in any way.

She craved it.

To be loved.

To love.

Sex.

Fucking.

All of it.

It was probably wrong for a twenty-one-year-old virgin to have an illicit affair, to be at the mercy and skill of an older man and to even fall in love, but it was what she wanted. She fantasized a lot about her future, even with this man in front of her.

Marco had featured in every single dream, and she wanted his touch more than anything else.

He reached out, and she tried so hard to hold her gasp as he stroked her cheek.

"You're here for one reason and one reason alone, to please me."

His words made her pussy wet. She wasn't embarrassed, humiliated, or upset. Why would she be? Marco was the man she had wanted.

"You're to be my Pet, Petal."

****

She wasn't running away screaming, and Marco considered that a plus. It never ended well if they were always screaming. He often found it really fucking annoying, not that he'd propositioned a woman like this before.

He fucked and left. That was his thing.

"What do I do then?"

"You wait for me."

"I wait for you?" she asked.

"This is your new home. You can do whatever you want. Have what you want." He pulled a credit card out of his wallet. "This is yours."

"I don't want your money."

"You'll get it all the same."

"So I'm going to be a whore."

"No."

"But by the very definition, I will be. You want to fuck me, and you're going to pay me for the pleasure."

He knew what he wanted to do with her dirty mouth and it was have those lips wrapped around his cock.

"A whore takes whatever client who wants her. I won't be sharing you. You'll belong to me. You won't be a whore. In a way, you'll be my wife."

"Your wife?"

"Yes. Without the need for a ring or any of that other bullshit people seem to like."

She stared down at the card. "This makes me a little uncomfortable."

"But knowing I want to have sex with you doesn't?"

"No."

He stared at her, even more intrigued. Glancing down, he admired her curves in the tight jeans and revealing top she wore. It was a camisole top with thin straps but molded to her body.

One of the straps was falling down her shoulder, and every couple of seconds, she moved it back up into place.

He wanted to peel her clothes off.

Why not have a look at the goods?

"Strip."

"Right now?"

"Yes."

She still held the credit card, and he stood back as she looked back at the windows.

"We're far enough up, no one can see us. You're safe." He would have to set some ground rules with her. There was no way he'd let anyone look at her or even glance at her. She belonged to him and only him.

He wasn't very good at sharing. Never had been.

She put the credit card on the nearest table, and then, working with her jeans first, she unsnapped the button.

He watched her as she swung her hips from side to side as she wriggled out of the jeans, kicking them off.

The torture was prolonged as she picked them up, folding them. He didn't need to know if she was neat or not. What he needed was for her to just get naked.

Next, she lifted up her camisole shirt, doing exactly the same as with the jeans, folding it neatly.

She stood before him in a pair of white ankle socks, an off-grey bra, and the same colored panties.

Ugly underwear aside, Marco didn't have a problem with her. She was fucking stunning.

"I said strip. I didn't say you could stop."

Her cheeks were red, but she didn't voice a complaint or ask him to stop.

He watched her, completely entranced.

She flicked the catch of her bra first, and she had beautiful, tight, red nipples. They were made for his mouth. She pulled her panties off, and then with her hands once again clasped in front of her, pressing those tits together, she kept her head bowed.

Like the perfect little submissive.

He'd called her pet, but he was no Dominant. He liked to fuck and use a little bondage, but he wasn't a master.

He grabbed her arms and moved her into the center of the room so he could get a good look at her.

Some men wouldn't want her, as she was on the larger side, but he had a thing for her curves. He wanted to get his hands all over her, to have her spread out for him, at his mercy, begging for his touch.

He wouldn't have cared if she was a virgin or not, but knowing no one else had touched her, well, that was one of the best fucking dreams in the world.

She would belong only to him. He took her

hands, lifting them up so he could see every single part of her.

"Do you like what you see?" she asked.

Marco walked around her. He placed a hand on her stomach, and he couldn't help but wonder what she'd look like swollen with his child. Avoiding her pussy and tits, he already saw how erect her nipples were, and the apartment wasn't cold.

He liked to keep it a certain temperature as he didn't like the cold himself.

Walking behind her, he placed a palm on her ass, feeling the curves.

She let out a little gasp as he slid his hand down her thighs, then up, inspecting her as a man would some kind of brood mare.

When he stepped back in front of her, he knew he'd pissed her off.

"I more than like." Taking her hand, he placed it on his rock-hard dick for her to touch. "Feel that. It's what you do to me every single time I'm in the same room."

He expected her to just hold him, to keep her palm resting on his dick. Petal was full of surprises as she began to rub him through his clothing. Slow at first, but then she gripped him tightly.

Not so tightly there was pain, but enough to know she wasn't afraid of him.

He liked it. He wanted more of it.

Stroking her cheek, he tilted her head back, wanting her lips. Just as he was about to take the kiss he wanted, his phone rang.

He sighed. "Duty calls."

Reaching into his pocket, he pulled away from temptation and went and dealt with business.

After all, business would always come first.

Chapter Two

One week later, Petal chopped up the vegetables to go into her stir-fry. It had been a week of being in the apartment with nothing to do but wait for Marco to arrive. He'd left unexpectedly and had yet to return.

Since he left her in the middle of his sitting room, naked, he'd not called or given her any details.

She'd made up her own entertainment, fed herself, and cleaned.

Her days were spent either cleaning, unnecessarily, any of his rooms, thoroughly, apart from his office and bedroom. She knew how much her father hated it when someone entered his zone and would often bitch if they even dared to step inside.

She wouldn't go into any of those personal places.

The last thing she wanted was to get shot. She didn't want to die, nor did she have any kind of death wish.

One day, she hoped to have a family of her own. It was a wish of hers and possibly even more far off than it was a week ago. Still, she would always hold out hope for her own happy ever after.

She drained the noodles and tossed them into the wok, giving them a good stir. Today she was really hungry, but she had made way too much.

"Lunch tomorrow."

Grabbing her bowl of food, she made sure the stove was turned off before heading into the dining room.

Marco lived in a rather luxurious apartment. It was spacious, and even as she was going stir crazy, it wasn't so bad most of the time. She had a small placemat for her meal as she didn't want to damage the wood of the table.

She used the chopsticks she had found and began to slurp up her food, enjoying the explosion of flavor on her tongue. Closing her eyes, she ate some more and paused when she heard the door opening.

Should she go and see who it was? Was it even Marco? Had someone come to kill her?

Her thoughts went rampant until she watched Marco enter the dining room. She couldn't speak as he looked at her. His gaze was on her and then the table.

It took her a few seconds to realize he was covered in blood.

"That smells good," he said.

"Erm, I have enough for us both."

He nodded.

"Wait, I think you should get cleaned up first."

"This isn't my blood."

"I gathered."

"I lost one of my men today."

"I'm so sorry."

He nodded.

She put her chopsticks down and went to him. There was not a part of him that wasn't covered with blood. Grabbing his hand, she walked him toward his room.

"May I go inside?" she asked.

"You've not been sleeping there?"

"I made up the spare room. I didn't want you to be mad."

"You'll sleep in my bed from now on."

"Noted." She entered his room, and he told her which door to open. She did so and walked into a bathroom. It was almost the same size as his bedroom.

Her guest bedroom and bathroom were much, much smaller. She didn't mind as she liked just having the space for herself.

She turned on the shower, and as it warmed up, she began to strip him down.

"Will these clothes need taking care of?" she asked.

"I'll deal with it."

"Okay."

She removed his clothes and tried not to stare at his heavily muscled, inked body. He was straight out of a bad boy magazine that fathers were always worried about their daughters falling for.

His cock stood out, long and thick. Even covered in blood, he was ready to fuck.

Petal didn't touch him though. She made sure not to touch him.

Opening the shower stall, she waited for him to get inside, and when he did, she was about to leave, but he caught her hand, dragging her into the shower.

He pressed her against the wall, taking her hands and holding them above her head.

Without another word, his lips were on hers.

The only part of him that wasn't covered by blood was his face.

Closing her eyes, she moaned as his body pressed against hers. His cock poked her stomach.

He was so big. When they had sex, at least the first time, it was going to hurt really bad. She whimpered as he bit her lip.

"I've thought about you all fucking week. Do you have any idea how hard it has been to stay away?"

"You don't have to stay away."

"It wasn't by choice, Pet." He kissed down to her neck. "I can't wait to fuck you. To know how you feel when you come all over my cock. For a woman that has been sold for pleasure, you don't seem to have a problem with it."

"I don't. Not when it comes to you."

"You want me too?"

She stared into his blue eyes and nodded. "Yes."

"You're still a virgin?"

"Yes."

"Yet you want this?" He pressed his cock against her stomach.

"Yes."

"It doesn't frighten you?"

"A little, but not enough to run screaming. I've been protected my whole life. Even now, I'm protected. I want to…" She stopped talking. What else could she say?

"Talk to me, Pet."

"I don't think I can."

"I won't let you come and I won't touch you."

"You're supposed to be washing away the blood."

"And it's doing a wonderful job."

He pulled off her shirt, and next unsnapped her jeans. She watched him kneel before her and couldn't help but wonder how many women he'd done that for. She couldn't imagine it was a whole lot.

Marco Guidi was the kind of man who didn't kneel for anyone.

He tore her panties off, throwing them aside. "From now on, you don't wear any of them, understand?"

"Yes."

"Good. I don't want anything in the way of what is mine."

She gasped as he put his hand to her pussy. This was really happening. It was finally going to be real. Petal only hoped she could survive it. The pleasure was already more intense than she could have ever hoped.

****

Work would always come first.

Marco was used to working his ass off, no matter the hour. The mafia didn't care if he'd been awake for forty-eight hours; if they needed him, he was there, no questions asked.

It was the way of his world, what he was used to, and he didn't have a problem with that most of the time.

Being called away from Petal that first day, he had wanted to kill a whole lot of people, and he had. He'd lost one of his best soldiers. The blood on him was from Luca, the man who'd died in his arms. From the time he was eighteen, Luca had been a good solider and one of the few men he trusted.

Watching him die had been heartbreaking.

The only thing to do after was to come home. There would be a lot more deaths, and a lot more pain before he finally found his own death. He had accepted that.

Men in his line of work, they often had a short life expectancy. There were always a rare few who were lucky, but staring into Petal's brown eyes, he would never have called himself lucky, until this very moment.

She was naked.

Most of the blood was off him.

One week he'd been thinking about spreading her thighs open and having his way with her. A full seven days of yearning, of wanting, of blue balls that drove him crazy. He'd never had blue balls, but he'd never waited for one woman to satisfy his appetite before.

Everything to do with Petal was all new to him.

No other woman would do. The only pussy he wanted was hers.

"You know you're all mine. You can't look at another man or have another man."

She smiled. "We've already been over this."

"Good." He grabbed the sponge and soap. "Clean me."

She took the items from him, and he watched as she lathered up the sponge before putting it on his skin. She worked the lather into his flesh, and the water ran it right off.

He couldn't look away, mesmerized by her.

From the moment he noticed her, he'd been addicted. She kept on working the lather into the sponge before washing him.

She had avoided his dick.

"Clean me." He took her hand and wrapped it around his length so she had no doubt as to what he meant. "Use your hand, not that thing."

She nodded but didn't say a word.

For all of her bravado, Petal was a little embarrassed. He saw the heat in her cheeks and couldn't help but smile.

"Never held a cock before, little virgin?"

"You know I haven't. It's what being a virgin is all about."

"A hymen can stay intact, Pet, even when you do other things."

"These hands haven't touched anyone else, and this body hasn't been touched by anyone. I'm a virgin in all things."

"Do you want to remain a virgin?" he asked, cupping her ass. He gave the rounded globe a squeeze, and she whimpered but didn't pull away.

"No."

"You don't?"

He watched as she licked her lips and shook her head.

"You want to know what it's like to ride a cock,

to be fucked, to be sated?"

"Yes." The single word was so faint, but he heard it. There was no doubt where it had come from.

She didn't avert her gaze, and he liked that she was willing to take what she wanted without backing down.

Letting go of her ass, he took the soap and sponge from her. He moved her into position so he could lather her body. She stayed perfectly still, but he saw her nipples and the flush to her body.

The loofah got in the way, and he soaped up his hand, touching her, washing her, getting her ready for him and him alone. He turned her so her back was then to him.

Marco took extra time with her ass. He loved touching her, and he couldn't get enough of this ass.

When they were both clean, he turned off the shower.

"What about our hair?"

"Another time."

Opening the shower, he wrapped a towel around his waist and then held one out for her.

Petal stepped into his arms, and he kissed her as he wrapped it around her body.

"Are you hungry?" she asked.

"Not just for the food you've cooked." Taking her hand, he led her back into his bedroom.

He stopped them both at his bed.

Gripping her towel, he pulled her close and slammed his lips down on hers. She melted against him, wrapping her arms around his neck and moaning his name as he broke from the kiss. Trailing his lips down, he pulled the towel from her body. He did have every intention of going straight to eat some food, but the bed, Petal … his desires wouldn't fade. He wanted her, and already denying himself the pleasure of her body for a week was enough to drive him crazy.

Pressing her down onto the edge of the bed, he nudged her back. She moved into position, and he held one of those large tits as he flicked the tip of her nipple with his tongue.

She moaned, and he sucked it into his mouth, loving the gasp and the deeper sounds of pleasure coming from her lips. They were addictive, and he couldn't get enough of them. He didn't want to ever have his fill of her. She was fucking incredible.

Sliding between her open thighs, he knew this first time wouldn't be the best for her, but he could make it perfect.

Petal was going to be addicted to his touch and want to be fucked by him repeatedly.

Chapter Three

Petal gripped the sheets beneath her, trying hard to focus on Marco and not get lost in the sea of pleasure. His mouth felt so good on her nipples. She closed her eyes, opened them again, and watched as he moved to the other breast, licking and sucking.

Marco pressed the mounds together, clearly not in any kind of hurry when it came to her body, and it drove her crazy because she didn't want him to stop what he was doing. It felt amazing, and she moaned his name, filling the room with her pleasured sounds.

"You're so fucking beautiful," he said.

He began to kiss down her stomach, and he spread her thighs. She didn't fight him as he worked her, holding her open for his touch.

When his hands slid over her pussy, she couldn't tear her eyes away from him. He stroked across her curls.

Her mother had advised her to completely shave it off, but she couldn't bring herself to do that.

"Do you want the hair gone?" she asked.

"No. I like this."

She cried out as he slipped a finger between her slit and touched her clit. That small touch was enough to have her coming off the bed.

Marco pressed a hand down on her stomach, keeping her in place. He moved down to her entrance and slid right back up to her clit, circling the bud.

"How does that feel?"

"Good."

"Really good?"

"Yes."

"It's about to get a whole lot better."

He moved between her thighs, and she'd read enough books to know what was coming next.

His tongue stroked across her clit, and she cried out, the instant pull of heat shocking her to her core.

She had touched herself many times, the books she'd read arousing her to the point she had no choice but to take care of herself. She was no stranger to an orgasm, but Marco touching her, licking her, it took the sensations to a whole new level, shocking her at just how amazing it felt.

He flicked her clit with his tongue before sucking it into his mouth. She wasn't going to be able to last much longer.

Her orgasm was already starting to build as he worked her nub like a pro. Marco knew what he was doing, and as she got close, he kept up the same motions of teasing her, drawing her pleasure to the edge, until she was finally thrown over, and it left her breathless.

His name was like a mantra coming from her lips.

Marco wasn't done. He moved up between her thighs, and she didn't have time to come down from her orgasm before his cock slid between them, the tip of him bumping her clit.

"This is going to hurt. I'm not going to pretend this won't be painful, but it will end."

She nodded.

What could she say to him exactly? There was nothing to be said. Words were useless to her.

His cock went to her entrance, and she had imagined this moment so many times. She didn't think it would be that painful, but as he slammed to the hilt, she was proven wrong. Marco didn't take her slowly.

He tore through her virginity, claiming it in one hard thrust that had her screaming. He covered her mouth with his hand, silencing her.

She stared into his eyes as her pussy felt on fire from his deep possession. She couldn't move. He was so big. It hurt a lot more than she anticipated. She didn't know what to do.

"I'm so sorry. I wish it didn't hurt. I don't ever want to hurt you."

His hand was still over her mouth, but as the seconds passed, maybe even minutes now, the pain began to ebb away. Marco still didn't move, and she was thankful of that. There was no way she wanted him to move right now.

From the books she'd read, she knew there was going to pain. It was considered part of the process, but to actually experience it, she didn't want to feel pain of any kind again. She was a wimp when it came to hurting. She didn't handle it well, and often cried. Her father would get angry because he hated to see any of his girls in pain.

Marco removed his hand, but she didn't scream.

Tears leaked out of the corner of her eyes, but so long as she didn't stop looking at Marco, everything was fine.

She could think and feel.

"Does it still hurt?" he asked.

She shook her head. The pain was gone. All she felt now was full. Full, and strange. She wanted to move, but fear of what it might feel like held her back.

"Do you trust me?"

"I don't know." Her voice didn't sound like her own.

"One day, you'll trust me."

She had no idea what to say to him about that. This was all new, and in the back of her mind, she wondered if he'd send her back once he had his fun, or whatever this was.

Pushing those thoughts away, she focused on him.

He began to pull out, and she reached out, grabbing his waist.

"Does it hurt?"

"No."

"Are you expecting pain?"

"Yes."

"Don't. Just let your body do all the work. Can you do that for me?"

She nodded. Talking right now seemed too hard for her. She just wanted to breathe, and not think about anything.

Marco pulled all the way out of her, and there was no pain. She didn't want him to leave, so she held him, hoping he'd stay deep inside her.

"You like that?" He began to slowly rock inside her.

"Yes."

"Good."

Marco took her hands, placing them either side of her head, and began to thrust inside her. He started off slow, and gradually, as she began to meet his thrusts, he started to fuck her. The pain transformed into the best kind of pleasure. She couldn't even begin to describe it.

Her body took over, and she wanted him to go harder, faster, to fuck her with everything he had and to never let her go.

Once he started, she didn't want him to stop.

When he came, she felt the pulse of his cock as he slammed in deep, and she knew she was never going to be the same again.

****

Marco wasn't used to taking care of a woman after fucking her. The women he'd been with all knew what to do, and afterward, left him alone.

Staring down at the blood on the sheets and his

cum dribbling out of Petal's pussy, he couldn't leave her. He didn't want to.

Running her a bath, he carried her through and gently lowered her into the water.

"You don't have to do this."

He noticed she didn't like too much attention and often shied away from his touch. She'd had no problem with his hands all over her during sex.

"I'm taking care of you."

"I know this is … weird. I can take care of myself."

He cupped her cheek, tilting her head back so she had no choice but to look at him. "I'm taking care of you. End of discussion."

What Petal needed to realize was he considered her part of his pleasure. She wasn't a chore or business.

She was what he'd been wanting for some time now.

His sweet little curvy virgin was no more, and he fucking loved that he was the first. He was going to be the *only* man between those sweet thighs. They had felt good wrapped around him. They were nice and juicy, and if he'd not been holding her hands, he'd have held those thighs, feeling the strength as he pounded away inside her.

He had a lot of plans for Petal.

"I'll be back. Just relax. If I don't find you doing that, I'll spank your ass."

Her cheeks were a beautiful shade of red, and he would have no problems when it came to turning her bottom the exact same color. Stroking her cheek, he kissed her again and went back to his bedroom.

The bloodstain shouldn't affect him.

In his world, that was a sign of a completed truce or deal. Marriage was never about love or emotions. It was always a business contract. Marco had simply taken what he wanted, struck a deal with her father, and now she was his in every way. Her father couldn't take her back, if he would even try, which Marco doubted he would.

She belonged to him.

Removing the sheets, he tossed them into the laundry basket and placed clean ones on the bed.

Petal had been his first virgin. He'd known she was going to hurt as he took her. Women always felt pain during their first sexual experience. He would give her a chance to heal, and once he knew she wouldn't be in pain again, she was going to have to get used to him being inside her.

Remembering the tightness of her sweet cunt, wrapped around him like a vise, he wanted to fuck her again. Only this time, he wanted her to come all over his dick.

Soon.

There was no reason for him to rush anything. All he wanted to do was spend time with Petal.

She was not a job he needed to complete. She was all about his pleasure. He walked into the bathroom and smiled as he saw Petal doing exactly as he asked.

"Hey, beautiful," he said.

"Hey. You think I'm beautiful?"

"Yes." He walked toward the bath, and he didn't even have to ask her to move. She made room for him behind her.

He'd never shared a bath or shower with any woman.

"How are you feeling?" he asked.

"I'm okay. A little sore but I'm okay." She leaned back against him. "I don't know what to expect with you."

"How do you mean?"

"Should I be afraid of you?" she asked, tilting her head back. "I don't know what you want from me."

"I want to enjoy you."

"For how long?"

"You think this has a time stamp?"

"I've never done anything like this. Is my dad expecting me back? Will you take me back to him? I don't know what to think or feel anymore." She rubbed at her temple.

He took her hands and kissed her head. "Stop worrying. Stop thinking of anything but enjoying our time together." She wasn't ready to hear that he intended to keep her for a long time. "You'll be living here. You don't have to cook or clean for me."

"And if I want to?"

"You can do whatever you want, but I do also pay someone."

"I like to cook at least. Cleaning is okay, but I do love to cook," she said.

"There will be days, even weeks when I won't be able to come here."

"Are you married?"

He laughed. "No. I'm not married."

She looked up at him. "Work?"

"Yes, I'll have to go for work. You can't come with me."

"I know. It's dangerous."

He stared down at her. "You know who I am, don't you?"

"Yes."

"When?"

"My dad tried to keep me locked in a cage, but that doesn't mean I *need* to be locked in a cage. I know what you do and who you are. I know you also bought me. Made a deal with my dad. I also know that I don't *care* what it is you do. I like being here with you." She sighed. "Sorry."

"You never said anything."

"Why would I?"

"Some women would have called the cops."

"I guess I'm not some women."

"No, you're not." He brushed his lips across hers. "You're something else entirely."

She chuckled. "What do you like to do on your downtime?"

"There is rarely any downtime for me, but I like watching movies when I can."

"What kind?"

He couldn't help but smile. "Are you trying to get to know me, Pet?"

"Maybe. Is that so hard?" she asked.

Marco was used to women wanting his credit card after taking his cock, not knowing more about him. He was going to have to get used to having Petal around and not expecting her to react like all the other women in his life.

She was different, and he needed to start treating her as such.

Kissing her again, he knew it wasn't going to be a challenge. He already loved spending time with her, and she was still nervous about being near him. That would all change. He'd make sure of it.

Chapter Four

Petal closed her eyes as she snuggled against Marco. After he'd taken her virginity, she had gotten him all to herself for three days before he had to leave again. He'd gotten a call that had taken him away from her.

She liked having him around, and now she had him back after two and a half weeks of not seeing him. There was a calendar in his bedroom, and she'd marked off the days.

He'd finally turned up on a Sunday.

The moment she saw him, she'd wanted to run into his arms, but she held herself back. She didn't know what he expected from her or what he hoped she'd do. All of this was new to her, and she found it so confusing at times.

Her parents had called her. Marco had left her a cell phone for them to get in touch, but it wasn't the same anymore as being with Marco.

He randomly sent guards to her to take the lists of things she required for them to shop for. She couldn't go out yet, and she'd been in the apartment now without leaving for nearly a month. She'd wanted to go out, but the moment Marco entered, all she wanted to do was snuggle up against him as he unwound from the day.

There *were* a couple of other things she wanted more, but for now, being against him, holding him, knowing he was alive, that was enough. It would have to do.

Every now and then, he'd kiss the top of her head and hold her arm a little tighter. She had glanced so many times at his cock, and all she wanted to do was ask him if he wanted to … experiment.

Her body had fully recovered.

She felt fine.

Perfect even.

Only she was horny in a bad way.

All she had been able to think about for days now was his cock, feeling him inside her. She'd wake up, covered in sweat from wet dreams, her pussy dripping with need.

It wasn't fair. He'd given a taste of what she could have, and now she wanted more of it, was hungry for everything he could give her.

She had read so much in her books and knew there was a lot more pleasure to be had between a man and woman, if only she knew how to draw him out.

It was … impossible.

What did she do to make him realize she wanted him?

"What's going on in that head of yours?" he asked.

"Nothing."

"You're doing a lot of fidgeting for nothing."

"I'm going to go and get us a drink. Do you want anything?" she asked. She didn't wait around for him to say anything and disappeared into his kitchen. Opening the fridge, she was very aware he'd followed her.

She stared at the open fridge as he pressed against her back.

"What is going on?" he asked.

"It's nothing." There was nothing going on with her. She wanted to touch him, explore him, and so much more but didn't have the first clue of how to tell him.

He gripped her arm, closed the fridge door, and pressed her against it. Her heart started to beat rapidly, and when he cupped her around the neck, tilting her chin up, she couldn't look away.

"Now, I know you're lying."

"I'm not lying."

"Your pulse says otherwise. I expect more from you, Pet. I don't want to have to work to figure out what is wrong with you. I've had a hell of a couple of weeks. Life is rather shitty right now, and you're the only ray of light I've got. I don't want to waste the time I've got with you over bullshit. Tell me what is wrong."

"It's … stupid."

"Now!" He growled the word, and it made her jump.

She was wasting time. It *was* stupid of her, and she hated that he yelled at her. Now, she was pissed.

Shoving him hard, she glared at him. "You may get what you want everywhere else. There is no reason to growl at me because I'm having a hard time telling you exactly what I want!"

He raised a brow.

"I'm not finished." She held her hand up. "I've been in this damn apartment, waiting for you to come back. I'm new at all of this, and you lose your temper with me?" She was pissed now, but still very much horny. "If you must know, Marco, I was thinking of a way of approaching sex with you. I don't know what to do. All I know is it has been a couple of weeks and I've thought about you nonstop. I want you, and that's why I'm freaking out. Do I just come out and say, 'Marco, I want you to fuck me'? What do I do?"

She took a deep breath and slammed a hand across her mouth when she realized she had kept on talking. She hadn't stopped, and now he knew the truth.

The raised brow lowered, and she saw the cocky grin return. He stepped toward her as she had shoved him away.

The fridge stopped any chance of her escaping, and she tilted her head back to look at him.

"You want to fuck, Pet?"

She nodded her head.

He placed a finger on her chin, slowly dragging it down her body, through the valley of cleavage to finally cup her pussy. She wore a pair of pajama bottoms, but it wasn't enough to protect her from his touch.

"You think all I wanted to do was watch a movie?"

"You put it on."

"I want you to be comfortable around me, Pet. The movie was a means to an end. I would gladly be fucking your sweet pussy right now, and all you had to do was ask." He picked her up and carried her out of the kitchen to their bedroom.

That wasn't so bad.

****

Dropping Petal down onto the bed, Marco grabbed her pajama bottoms, which were cute little ducks, and pulled them right off. She wasn't wearing any panties, and he sent a little prayer to whoever was watching him because they clearly gave a shit about him.

Spreading Petal's thighs, he stared down at her pussy. He'd been dreaming about this ever since he'd left her. The last thing he wanted to do was to be anywhere but with her. Still, when duty called, he had no choice but to respond.

He touched her pussy, stroking her wet flesh. Sliding a finger deep inside her, he felt how tight she was. He added a second finger and watched her cunt as he started to stretch her open, wanting her ready to take all of his cock. He pushed his thumb to her clit and began to stroke from side to side, feeling her answering pulse as she gripped his fingers tightly.

"You're the only person I thought about all fucking day, Petal. It was hard not to tell everyone to fuck off and deal with their own problems so I could come home and fuck you. You're all I want." He pulled his fingers from her pussy and sucked them into his mouth.

He closed his eyes as the taste of her exploded on his tongue. She was fucking amazing.

Gripping her thighs, he pressed his face against her pussy, licking and sucking at her clit before moving down to fuck her with his tongue.

She screamed his name, and he reached up, gripping her tits, squeezing them.

"Yes, fuck yes. Marco, please don't stop," she said.

It was the best sound in the world. He was more than pleased her parents hadn't made her too sweet. Hearing "fuck" spill from her lips turned him on. He didn't want her to be ashamed of her own desires and relished exploring them with her, when she was ready, of course.

"You drive me wild," he said, kissing up her body.

"Why did you stop?" she asked, ending on a moan as he kissed her.

"You're going to come around my cock." He reached between them. Holding his cock to her entrance, he stared into her eyes, and this time, he was slow as he filled her. He took his time, sinking inside her inch by glorious fucking inch. She squeezed him so tight, and it felt amazing.

He didn't want to stop. On the last few inches, he slammed in deep and heard her gasp.

"You're not in pain?"

"No, it feels wonderful."

He lifted her legs so they wrapped around his waist. Next, he locked his fingers with hers, putting her hands beside her head so he had complete control. She was spread open, at his mercy as he began to rock inside her. He worked his cock so he touched her clit, that little bud of nerves that made a woman go wild.

Marco loved watching her as she came undone on his dick.

In and out, he took his sweet time. He didn't even know where his patience had come from because all he wanted to do was fuck her hard and take her deep.

Right now, he wanted to feel every single ripple and pulse of her cunt as she took him. She had the tightest pussy, and it was the best.

Taking possession of her lips, he listened to her moan.

When he couldn't take it anymore, he moved up, going to his knees and having Petal rest her ass against his thighs. He stared down at where they were connected and slid his fingers through her slit, touching her pussy.

He felt her quiver as he teased her nub, stroking her. She was so wet for him, and he wanted to feel her come all over his cock.

"Come for me, Pet. Show me how much you've missed my dick."

It didn't take her long to find her peak, and even before she'd come down from her orgasm, he grabbed her legs and started to pound inside her. His dick was wet from her arousal, and he was so hard.

The sounds of their fucking filled the air. She cried his name, and he was never going to get tired of this.

"Yes, yes, please, it feels so good."

He fucked her harder. The bed slammed against the wall with the force of his thrusts. He filled her once more, going to the hilt as he came, flooding her womb with his cum. Wave upon wave of his release spilled inside her. He was shocked by how much he actually came, but this *was* what he'd wanted.

He loved watching Petal, the way her tits bounced, the feel of her curves wrapped around his body.

Even her pussy was a dream, and he couldn't give her up, not ever.

"I missed you," he said, smiling down at her.

She chuckled. "I missed you too."

He looked into her eyes and wondered if she was just copying what he was saying or if she truly really meant what she said.

Stroking her cheek, he couldn't help but yearn for the truth to have spilled from her lips. He wanted her more than anything, and that was never going to change.

Kissing her lips, he bit down on her bottom one and loved her moan. "From now on, you tell me the truth. You want to fuck, you tell me we're going to fuck, and we will. You don't hold back. You don't pretend. We will fuck. Whatever you want, wherever you want it. I live to serve your hungry pussy." He kissed her again so she wouldn't argue with him.

Her mouth was the next thing he wanted on his dick, but for now, he couldn't get enough of her pussy.

Chapter Five

Petal ran her hands up and down Marco's thighs. She knelt on the floor in front of him and waited for further instruction. He'd been hers for twenty-four hours, and she wasn't going to waste a moment with him.

"You've got this look in your eye. What do you want?" he asked.

"I want to … lick you?"

"You do?"

She glanced down at his cock and saw it outlined in his suit pants. Her mouth watered. She had read about sucking a man's cock, and Marco had a very nice one. She wanted to give him the same kind of pleasure he gave her.

"Yes."

"You ever sucked a man's dick before?"

"You know I haven't." She loved being a virgin in all things, especially as it drove Marco crazy. He loved the fact no other man had ever touched her. She belonged to him, and now no one else would get to touch her.

He reached down, stroking a curl of her brown hair behind her ear.

"You got yourself down there. Show me what you've got."

"I don't know what I'm doing."

"You're being a little tease now. You know you've got to get my dick out first. Do it."

She wanted to suck him, to be more experienced with him, but it was still a little … embarrassing. She didn't know what she was doing, and she didn't want to spoil anything.

"I'll make it easy for you." Marco released his belt, sliding the leather out of the loops. "The rest is up to you."

He rested his head on his hand.

At first, she'd thought he was bored, but she had come to realize quite quickly that Marco wasn't bored. He just liked to watch her. She'd noticed it all those times he came to her father's. Whenever she was around, his gaze would always be on her, and she liked it.

Even as her hands shook, she worked his button open. This had to be the first time he had a woman nervous to pleasure him.

He wasn't forcing her.

She wanted this.

She slid the zipper down, the sound seeming to echo in the room. She sat back.

"He's not going to crawl out of there. You're going to have to touch me."

She took a deep breath and reached into his pants, taking hold of his cock. He was rock-hard, and as she gripped him, he let out a hiss. She immediately let him go, not wanting to hurt him.

"It's okay. I'm just having to get used to you."

"I don't want to hurt you."

"It doesn't hurt. I want to fuck you so badly. Your mouth will have to do." His smile had her stomach flip.

She didn't know how he managed to make her feel so much. He had to have a gift. She took hold of his dick again, easing it out of his suit pants. He let out a groan, and this time, she didn't stop until she finally had him exposed.

His cock stood out, long and wide.

"You've got him now, Pet. You're going to have to deal with him."

Nibbling the corner of her mouth, she was suddenly overcome with nerves.

"Lick the tip," he said.

She pressed her tongue to the head and licked him.

"Don't stop. Now, go down the sides." She did as he said. Closing her eyes, she started to lick his cock. "Good, good. Now, take me in your mouth."

She sucked the tip of his cock, only she didn't stop, sliding her mouth over the length of him until he hit the back of her throat. She pulled up and slid down, bobbing her head, moaning around his length.

"Fuck, that's it. Yes, you've got it right."

Opening her eyes, she looked up to see Marco watching her. He sank his fingers into her hair, and gripped her tightly, guiding her over his length. He thrust up, causing her to gag, and she loved it, wanting him to go deep, to fuck her throat, exactly how he wanted to.

She worked her mouth over him, covering his cock in her saliva.

Marco held her face as he rocked into her mouth, and she swallowed him down. She knew he wasn't going to hurt her, and she loved what he was doing, and giving him this pleasure.

She reached between her thighs, touching her clit. Whenever she was with Marco, she was always in a permanent state of arousal. He made her ache in all the right ways.

"Are you touching yourself?" he asked.

She hummed her response, and it only made him curse and thrust up into her mouth a little harder.

"You drive me fucking crazy. Shit, I'm not going to last. If you don't want to swallow my cum, you're going to have to stop."

This was about his pleasure. Petal wanted to feel him spill into her mouth.

When he came, he did so with a growl. His cock seemed to get bigger as he filled her mouth, spilling his cum inside her.

She had no choice but to swallow as there seemed to be so much of it. She milked him for every single drop.

Only when he was done did he collapse on the bed.

She licked her lips.

"Did you come?" he asked.

She shook her head.

Petal gasped as he lifted her up, and his face suddenly pressed between her thighs. He licked at her pussy, bringing her to an orgasm and licking at her juices as she came hard. By the time he was finished, she was the one panting for breath.

"I can't believe I wasted all those years."

"What years?" she asked.

"I should have taken you when you turned eighteen." He crashed his lips down on hers, and to Petal, it was the most romantic thing he'd ever said to her.

****

"You don't have to stay in the apartment forever," Marco said, leading Petal down to the indoor swimming pool.

It had been over a month since he'd taken Petal for his own, and he realized she hadn't gone anywhere or done anything. He'd offered to take her shopping, but she had no interest in buying clothes.

Instead, he presented her with a bikini, one that showed off her curves. She'd been so nervous, and he had to pull her hands away from her body so he could get a good look at her. Even now as they stood in the elevator, she kept trying to hide behind him.

He let go of her hand, holding her against his side with an arm around her waist.

"You're doing this on purpose," she said, glaring

at him.

"You've got nothing to hide."

"Easy for you to say."

"If you even for a second comment on your size, elevator or not, I will spank your ass."

"I'm used to people pointing, okay? I was bullied in school."

"The all-girls' school?" he asked.

"Yes, does that surprise you? I wasn't thin or tiny, and they loved to point it out every single day how ugly I am."

Marco dropped the towels he was holding and pressed her up against the corner of the elevator. The pool would be free and clear because his men would have cleared the pool. This building was owned by him, so he got first pick of all the facilities. He wasn't going to be sharing his woman and her body with anyone else. Her curves were for him and him alone.

Slamming his lips down on hers, he pressed his cock against her core.

Breaking from the kiss, he trailed his mouth down to her ear, biting on her lobe until she groaned. "You feel that?" he asked.

"Yes."

"All you ever need to think about is how *I* feel. I love your curves, and I think you're the most beautiful woman in the world. If I ever see or meet these women who hurt you, know their days are numbered."

"You can't go around killing people who have hurt me."

"I can't?"

"Marco?"

"You're mine, Pet. Every single part of you. Those tears are mine; you are mine. I'll brand your entire body so you know you belong to me." He kissed her again, hard. "Those women need to learn a lesson. You don't hide. You stand tall and proud. I love your body. Me, no one else. You care about what *I* want. Understand?"

"Yes, Mr. Bossy."

"You need someone bossy in your world." The elevator doors opened. "It's time for us to go for a swim."

He wrapped his arm around her, walking out to the pool.

"No one is here," she said.

"Exactly. It's just you and me. Unless you want company?"

"You can organize people to come for a swim to make me feel happy?"

"Yes. I'll get my guards to jump in the pool. They won't look at you."

"You'd really do that for me?" she asked.

"You need to realize there is a hell of a lot I would do for you." Marco knew it was only a matter of time before he was called away again. This was his business. The life of a Capo meant he didn't have the luxury of calling into work sick, or taking a holiday. This was his life, one he relished every single day of the week.

Hurting people, killing them in the name of the mafia, didn't bother him. He was used to the kind of violence he lived. He'd trained all of his life, and he was one of most feared men in the city.

Then there was Petal.

He'd never had a weakness. Over the years he'd known men who were total lethal bastards but had one woman who completely tore them apart. Their woman was their weakness, and they were too foolish to keep that shit to themselves. When their women were taken, or hurt, they didn't think through what they were supposed to do, so they made mistakes and got themselves killed or worse, just their women. He'd seen them fall apart not long after the death of their loved one.

Petal had changed him.

Without even realizing it, she'd gotten under his skin, and now, she was his weakness. Picking her up, he threw her into the pool. She let out a scream just before she hit the surface. He dived in, swimming toward her.

She broke the surface, pushing her hair out of her face.

"What the hell?"

He wrapped his arms around her, kissing her, keeping her completely off balance. Picking her up, he gripped her ass.

"You were saying something about hell?" He teased across the seam of her panties.

"I ... why did you throw me into the pool?"

"Because I wanted to."

"Is it always going to be like this?" she asked, cupping his face.

"Like what?"

"This. With you?"

"You tell me? What are you feeling?"

"Like we're the only two people left in the world."

"We're not. I want to keep you locked away in my tower like the princess you are, but I can't. I'm going to have to take you out."

"You won't."

"I will. I won't have you get sick because I'm confining you." He slid his finger under the material of her panties and started to stroke her pussy. "It doesn't mean we can't have a lot more fun though."

"Will you get rid of me?" she asked.

Her hands around his neck tightened a little more.

"Get rid of you?"

"Yes. Is this forever? Will you get bored of me?" She wanted security.

"I'll never get bored of you. This is forever."

"I can live with that."

She pressed her lips against his, and he knew there wasn't any other woman in the world who'd ever be able to compare to her.

Chapter Six

Marco kept to his word, and a couple of days later, he took her out for lunch. He hadn't been called away, and Petal loved having his undivided attention. The restaurant was particularly nice, the kind that made her nervous as everyone looked like they wore million-dollar outfits just to sit and enjoy a coffee.

"You look stunning," he said, reaching over the table and taking her hand.

In the short time they'd been out of his apartment, she'd noticed a difference in his demeanor. He didn't touch her as much, and he always had a hand ready to grab his weapon. She missed his sweet touches and the charming flirtation he always had with her.

"I don't really fit into a place like this." Her father had been a wealthy man, not overly so, but he'd taken care of all of them. This was out of her comfort zone though.

"You don't need to fit in. No one here needs a reason or an excuse as to why you're here. Own who you are, and they are beneath you."

"Do you do that? Make yourself believe they're all beneath you?" she asked.

"For the most part, they are. I own this place. I own most of the major establishments in this town. If I'm unhappy, I make sure the people who made it so, feel my anger."

"It must be hard though. You've got to learn to trust people close to you."

"I don't trust anyone."

"No one?" she asked.

"No. In my world, you trust the wrong person you're dead."

"You don't feel lonely?" She was finding it hard

not to feel a little upset by his words. She trusted him. Her father didn't even give her a choice in trusting Marco. She'd been passed off to him.

"No, it's not lonely. I'm alive."

"Excuse me." She cut him off, and without waiting for permission, she left the table, heading toward the bathroom.

No one else was there, and she went straight to the sink, gripping the edge. She closed her eyes, counting to ten. When that didn't work, she counted again.

"Stupid. Stupid. Stupid." She shouldn't be hurt because he didn't trust her. Marco had made it plain he didn't trust anyone.

The door opened, and she looked up to find Marco inside the women's bathroom.

"You're in the wrong room."

"I'm in the right room. You know, I've never had a woman just get up and leave."

She turned to give him her full attention. "I'm not trying to be difficult here."

"What did I say?" he asked.

She opened her mouth, about to lie to him, but he held his hand up.

"Think before you speak, Pet. Remember what I told you about lying."

She sighed. "Fine. You don't trust anyone. I've never given you a single reason to doubt me."

"You've never given me a single reason to trust you."

"I've known who you are from the very beginning."

"You have?"

"I'm not an idiot. I really wish you and my dad would stop treating me like I am. I know you're part of—" She pressed her lips together, trying to find the right words. "A certain group of people. I could have betrayed you long ago. What about the other night when I helped you shower?" She felt the tears in her eyes, and she turned her back, not wanting him to see her tears as weakness, even if that was exactly what they were.

She tensed up as he held her arms. His lips brushed across her neck.

"I've never been able to trust anyone in my life, Pet. With you, I don't know what the fuck I'm doing. I want to be the kind of man you deserve."

She looked at the mirror, staring at him. "What kind of man do I deserve?"

"One who can give you everything."

"You can't?"

"There will always be limits. You'll never be able to go to work, or have a regular life. Walks in the park won't come without consequences. There will always be people around us, watching us. Waiting for me to fail. You will always be at risk."

"Getting on a bus comes with risks. Walking down a street comes with risks. Even getting on a plane. There are risks all over the place. I could die without any of your enemies or friends raising a hand. It's the world, Marco."

"I will protect you."

His arms wrapped around her.

Resting her hand on top of his arms, she took a deep breath. This man. This crazy, intense, insane man, had a way of making her feel so torn on everything.

She leaned back against him, and his lips danced across her skin.

Love was a feeling she wasn't used to.

Marco was the man she'd been falling for. There's no way she could love him already, was there?

"Are you hungry?" he asked.

Her stomach answered for her, letting out a growl.

He laughed against her skin. "I'll take that as a yes. It has never been my intention to hurt you, Pet. I'm used to not having anyone. You're above everyone else. You're the one person who could destroy me without doing anything."

"I would never rat."

"If you were to die, that would destroy me."

"Oh."

"Yes. I want you for the rest of my days, Pet. Not just to satisfy my hunger." He kissed her cheek. "That's enough for today. It's time we headed back outside. I want to feed you before you get too hungry." He grabbed some tissues and dabbed under her eyes. "No more crying for me. Please. I can't stand to see your tears."

****

Biting Petal's ass, Marco heard her cry out. He spread the cheeks of her ass, staring at her glistening cunt and tight, puckered hole. He'd already come deep inside her pussy, and their combined releases were dripping out onto the bed.

Sliding his fingers through her slit, he touched her clit, and she pushed back against him, losing all of her inhibitions.

"Yes."

"You want my dick again?"

"Yes, please."

"Tell me what you want," he asked.

"Fuck me, Marco, please, fuck me."

He loved it when she talked dirty. It didn't matter how many times he took Petal; each time was always better than the last.

She didn't hold back. Her passions matched his own, and especially as she didn't feel any pain like their first time, anything he wanted she was more than willing to give.

He slid his cock back inside her. Even though he'd fucked her twice already and she was full of his cum, it was still a tight fit. He gripped her hips, watching her pussy suck his cock inside.

They were a perfect fit.

Slamming to the hilt, he held himself deep, feeling her tighten around him, before easing out until only the tip remained inside. She whimpered his name, and he fucked her, pounding hard and deep, making her take all of it, before slowing down.

She released a growl, and the sound was beautiful music as he teased her.

Her puckered little asshole was calling to him, begging to be touched. He spat down on that tight hole and moved his fingers over her forbidden entrance.

She tensed up, and he held himself still within her.

"What are you doing?"

"You've read all of those dirty books. You know exactly what I'm doing and what I want to keep on doing to you." He slid his fingers over her asshole, teasing her, getting her excited and comfortable at his touch.

Finally, he pushed against that tight entrance, and the muscles kept him out. Nothing ever told him no, and certainly not muscles.

Pressing forward, he sank the tip of his finger into her anus and heard her gasp. The sound was sweet music, but he wasn't even done yet. He kept moving his finger in and out, making sure she took more of him until the entire finger was in her ass.

He added a second finger, stretching her.

"It's too much!"

"Is it? Touch your pussy. Let's see if you have a

problem then."

She started to rock back against the finger in her ass the instant she touched her clit. He worked his two fingers, stretching her, getting her ready for his dick.

When he couldn't take anymore, he slid his fingers from her ass and eased his cock out of her dripping pussy. He loved seeing her full of his cock, the white streams falling from her hole.

Now, he wanted to flood her asshole.

Petal made him very possessive, and he wanted to mark her, fill her with his scent, so every single man that came into contact with her would know he was the one who fucked her. Crazy how he felt, but that was what he wanted more than anything.

She tensed up again as he placed the tip of his very large cock against her anus.

"Keep playing with your pussy. Don't stop. Relax."

He knew it was hard for her, but he took his time, pressing the tip of his cock into her ass and slowly pushing more inside her. She didn't stop working her clit, and he slowly rocked within her, letting her get accustomed to the new feelings.

Her ass was even tighter than her pussy.

Marco held onto her hips, squeezing as she finally took all of him inside her. They fit perfectly together.

"How are you feeling?" he asked, leaning over her and brushing his lips against her neck.

"Full."

"Is it too painful? Do you want me to stop?" He didn't want to, but if she couldn't handle it anymore, he'd stop for her. He wanted her to enjoy this, not to hate it.

"No, don't stop. It's weird but not too bad."

"You can handle it?"

"I can handle whatever you want to give me."

"That's my girl," he said. He bit down on her neck, knowing how much she loved him doing that. He licked over her pulse to soothe out the bite of pain. "I want you to come for me. Come on my cock and then I'll fuck this ass just the way you want me to."

She worked her clit, and he heard the wet sounds from her touches. He loved her needs and desires. They matched his own, and she never said no to anything. She wasn't afraid to either. He didn't want a submissive doll. Petal was more than he could have ever hoped her. He adored her fire and passion.

Her body though—she was fucking stunning. He'd always had a thing for curvy women, but Petal, she was everything to him.

"I'm going to come!"

"Do it. On my cock."

She cried out, and he groaned, feeling her ass squeeze him tighter in time to the pulse of her orgasm.

It was amazing, and even before she came down from her peak, he was thrusting inside her asshole.

He continued to kiss her neck, driving her arousal higher as he fucked her anus.

Petal started to push onto his dick, taking more of him inside her. He didn't lose control as this was her first time and he intended to spend a lot of time working her ass, playing her, pleasing her, fucking her.

Whenever he thought about the future, he always came back to her. Their time together.

Marco knew he was in love with her and had been for a couple of years now but had never given himself the chance to truly show it. She was his world, and now he couldn't think of having a day without her in it.

She was more than a mistress, more than a fuck.

She was everything.

He came hard inside her ass, wrapping his arms around her, knowing he couldn't let her go. He didn't want to.

Chapter Seven

"You seem happy enough," her mother said.

Petal glanced over at her mother. Marco had business to do, and much to her surprise, he'd taken her along with him. She pushed some of her hair out, accepting the drink of water. Her stomach had been a little off the past couple of days.

She'd been with Marco nearly two months now. He did still have to leave her, but he didn't take weeks, like he did in the early days of their relationship. Each night, he came back to her, no matter how late it was.

"I am happy," she said.

"I'm glad. I was shocked when your father made the agreement with Marco, but that's your father. I know you'll be a good girl. You always have been. I did expect Marco's tastes to be a little different."

Her mother liked to constantly point out Petal wasn't like other women. She didn't have a stick-thin frame, and her curves were just too obvious.

"Marco likes me the way I am, and I like me. I'm happy. He makes me so happy, and I know I make him so."

"Yes, I did notice. In all the years Marco has been coming here, I've never seen him smile. Today was the first time. You're good for him."

Her mother loved her in her own way. She just had a set of beliefs, and one of those was men didn't like a curvy woman.

Marco loved her curves, and what was more, she loved her own curves.

"I need something to eat," she said. Her stomach was really giving her a few problems.

"There's some salad in the fridge."

Petal stood up and paused as a wave of dizziness

swept over her. The floor started to sway. She took a step, and as she did, everything went dark.

****

Sounds.

Voices.

Words.

None of them made sense.

Petal opened her eyes.

Her mother, father, and Marco were standing over her.

"What is it? What happened?"

"The doctor is on the way." She turned her head to see her brother coming out of the living room.

Marco wrapped an arm around her waist, helping her to her feet. "What is going on?" she asked.

"You fainted," her mother said.

She looked toward Marco. The worry in his eyes was clear.

"I'm taking you to lie down."

"No, no, I should be fine."

"I'm not asking you." In front of her parents and siblings, Marco picked her up in his arms and began to carry her through to the bedroom.

"You really don't need to do this. I think you're overreacting just a little bit."

"I'm not. A woman doesn't just faint for no reason. You've not had a fall."

"I've been feeling a little sick."

"Sickness doesn't lead to fainting. It leads to diarrhea from bad food or a stomach bug."

"That's a colorful description," she said.

He placed her down on the bed, and she sat up. He pushed her back down again. She was no match for his strength.

"Marco, come on. I can book an appointment

with the doctor."

"One I trust is already coming here."

"So you trust someone now?" she asked, wanting to change the subject and teasing him.

"Don't, Petal. Not right now."

"What's wrong? I'm only kidding."

"I'm fine."

"Fine people don't just faint for no reason. You're getting checked over."

"Marco, please."

"No!" He leaned in close. "Don't you see, I can't have anything happening to you."

"Nothing is going to happen to me."

"I couldn't stand for it. I love you too much. There's no way I could ever—"

"You love me?" she asked, interrupting him.

There was no way she had heard that right. He said he loved her.

"Of course I love you. Could you have any doubt?"

"You never said anything."

"I'm … I'm a fucking fool when it comes to you, Pet. Such a damn fool. I love you more than anything. Why do you think I'd take you? I wanted to have you for so long, but I found every single excuse I could find not to have you."

She couldn't control her tears. "I can't believe you love me. I've hoped and prayed that you did."

"You wanted me to love you?"

"Yes. I love you more than anything. I want to spend the rest of my life with you. There's no one else I would ever want to be with."

"Marry me," he said.

"Yes."

He cupped her face and slammed his lips down

on hers. She moaned, wrapping her arms around his neck, holding him close.

"I'm not ever going to leave you or let anything happen to you. I love you. There's no way I could be without you."

Someone cleared their throat.

"Get the fuck out!" Marco yelled at whoever had invaded their privacy.

She cupped his cheek. "I think that was the doctor. I don't need a doctor."

"For me, you do. I need to know you're okay. That we're okay."

"As long as I have you, I know we'll be okay." She kissed his lips. "I didn't know I could feel this happy."

He kissed her again. "I love you."

"I love you too."

"The doctor?"

"I'll see him." She nodded.

"You think that was a request?" Marco winked at her. "I'll go get him."

She sat up and watched him walk out of the room. In love.

Finally, Marco Guidi belonged to her and she to him. There was no way she could ever be happier. This man was everything, and whatever life threw at them, she could survive it with Marco.

Epilogue

Eight months later

Marco stared down at his resting wife. She had just been through three hours of labor, and she looked exhausted.

"Hey," she said.

"Hey yourself. You're not too tired to hold her?" he asked, looking at his little girl.

Petal's reason for fainting had been that she was pregnant and dehydrated. The doctor had advised rest and to make sure she had a steady diet and fluids.

Hearing his woman was pregnant had been what Marco had wanted. He married her within two weeks, and he hired only the best men to take care of her. He had a weakness, but there was no way he'd let anyone see how much.

Stroking her hair back from her cheek, he felt like he'd aged twenty years during her labor.

She'd been in so much pain. His hands had cramps from her holding them as she pushed down, trying to get their little girl out.

"She is so perfect," Petal said.

The love he had for this woman and his little girl scared him. Ever since the ultrasound had revealed it was a girl, he'd been making sure there was no risk to his family. Petal made it a lot easier for him as she didn't mind staying by his side.

Kissing the top of his little girl's head, he rested his face against her neck. "You scared the shit out of me," he said.

"But we got through it. You told me labor wasn't that big of a deal. You've been shot enough times to know what real pain is like."

"I'm an asshole, and I don't know what I'm talking about." She was a fighter and one of the strongest women he'd ever known.

"Marco?"

"Yeah?"

"I love you so much."

"I love you too."

His little girl opened her eyes. They were the brightest blue. She made a little noise, and it just melted his heart.

"What should we call her?" he asked.

"I don't know. She is just so perfect in every single way."

"Anna," he said. "I want to call her Anna."

"Anna Guidi. I like it."

He kissed his wife, and he saw she was getting tired.

"Will you take her?" she asked. "You need to support her head."

Marco took his little girl, holding her in his arms. He stared down at her beautiful face.

"You don't need to be too stiff. She wants to feel loved and protected."

He held her closer.

"That's it, Daddy," Petal said.

He looked at her, amazed.

"You're a daddy now."

"A husband and a father," he said. "Wow."

He heard her giggle.

"I'm tired."

"You go to sleep. I'll be here to keep an eye on the two of you."

Petal nodded, her eyes falling closed. He heard her sigh.

"Marco?" she asked.

"Yes, baby."

"Do you want another one?" she asked.

"You went through all of that and you want another?"

"A brother or sister for Anna."

He lifted her hand to his lips, kissing her knuckles. "You're going to be the death of me, woman."

"Is that a yes?"

"You know I'll give you whatever you want. You just got to say the word."

"I want another child. I want to have a big family with you."

"We'll work on it soon." He held her hand and kept Anna tucked closer against his chest. When the nurse came in, she didn't say a word.

He wasn't leaving his girls. This was where he was meant to be.

Loving them.

Protecting them.

Making sure their lives were complete and perfect.

He didn't need anything else because they made his world worth everything.

The End

SAM CRESCENT

USING THE BIKER

Curvy Women Wanted, 16

Sam Crescent

Copyright © 2019

━◦•◆•◦━

Chapter One

"I'm telling you, the best way to get over that lying, fucking, cheating dickwad is to find a guy that is hotter, sexier, and will do a lot more kinky shit with you."

Josephine Lovell looked over at her excited friend, Mandy.

"You've brought me to a biker bar. Why?"

"I told you, these guys know how to party, and I know just the kind of guy to get you over dickface."

She couldn't help but laugh at Mandy's constant use of the word "dick" to describe Mitch, her very assholey ex-husband. The paperwork was signed, and she still had the house and the car, as well as a small alimony. Not that she needed it. She was more than happy to earn her keep, but her lawyer felt aggrieved for her, and so forced the alimony issue, especially as she'd put Mitch through college to become the esteemed lawyer he was today.

"And doing this at a biker party?"

"Yes, this is a celebration of one of their prospects finally earning their patch. There are no children around, and things are about to get so fucking real. I can't wait."

Mandy had been coming to these parties ever since she started working for the biker, Doc. No other name. It was the name he was known as, that and as the President of the Nowhere Men MC. They had decided to settle in their small town of End Valley. Yeah, she found it rather ironic that the Nowhere Men settled in End Valley.

She wasn't going to say anything. Mandy loved working for them in their garage they owned across town. They were far better than the local guy, Wilson, who liked to overcharge for shitty work.

Mitch always went to Wilson and always complained but refused to go to the bikers' garage.

He always said they were a bunch of thugs and criminals.

Mitch fucking his secretary flashed through Josephine's mind, and she squared her shoulders. As her ringless finger told the story, she was no longer married. The love she'd had for Mitch had certainly withered and died during the divorce, not to mention the long truth of his infidelity.

Her husband couldn't keep his dick in his pants, and now she wasn't going to keep her pussy from having some fun, especially as it had been over a year since she last had sex.

"You're right. I should be here. I'm allowed to be here."

"See, I told you. You need to get that idiot dick-fuck out of your life, and you need to start living again."

Mandy had never liked Mitch. From the very beginning, her best friend had a very one-sided view of Mitch, and now Josephine really wished she'd paid attention a whole lot more.

"I need to introduce you to Doc."

"No, no, no."

"You want to meet him."

"Mandy, I want to just relax, and let the night unfold. You think we can do that?"

"You're chickening out."

"No, I'm not. Really. I don't want you to throw me at some random guy." She pulled Mandy in for a hug. "I'm going to get a drink. You want anything?"

"Sure, sure."

She gave Mandy a kiss on the cheek and turned to leave. They had been best friends since kindergarten. Where most girls followed their boyfriends to college, Josephine, or Jo as she preferred to be called, had followed Mandy. Her best friend.

Josephine hadn't gotten into college. With a deadbeat father and mother, she had spent most of her later high school years working. That had taken a toll on her education, and she was lucky to have come out graduating at all. She didn't make the kind of numbers and scores Mandy made. So while Mandy studied, Jo worked, hoping to one day get that second chance where she could make a difference of some kind.

Then she met Mitch.

Her focus became him and helping him through college, all the time making up lame ass excuses to where she was now thirty-five and had finally enrolled in a night course.

She couldn't even believe she'd waited this long.

They didn't have any kids as Mitch didn't want them, and had often told her he didn't want to share her with anyone. All the time it had just been another element of his endless control over her life.

He told her what to wear, who to talk to, how to act. She had always made the excuse he loved her in his own way, but the truth was, he was a fucking dick. No wonder Mandy liked to call him that.

All of her adult life so far had been about a selfish, cheating, asshole who had fought every single part of their divorce. He'd even asked her to extend their relationship to that of an open marriage.

When she had thought about the fact she had actually considered it, she was sickened. A marriage was for life, not to be with other people. At least, *her* marriage was going to be that way. She didn't judge anyone their views and how they made their relationship work.

"You're at the bar! You've still not been served. Slick, come on, give a girl a break," Mandy said with a huge smile on her face. "Jo, I'd really like you to meet someone."

She'd been so consumed with her thoughts, she hadn't seen or heard Mandy approach, and she certainly didn't see who she was holding.

"Doc, I want you to meet my best friend in the entire world, Josephine Lovell, but you can call her Jo. It's what all the good guys get to call her."

Mandy had thrust a guy in his late forties in front of her.

She stood up, feeling mortified at her friend's lack of anything.

Doc didn't look embarrassed or upset.

"Pleasure to meet this mysterious woman. Mandy talks about you a lot," Doc said.

His voice was rough, like he did a lot of shouting, but it had that arousing edge to it.

"Will you look at that. I really need to go and dance. I have it booked in. Have fun, kids." Mandy left them alone.

Josephine was going to kill her best friend.

****

Doc had seen Jo's pictures a few times. Mandy had been blunt when it came to her views on his single self and her best friend.

"I'm so sorry. Mandy doesn't exactly do subtlety."

"She's charming." All the photos he'd seen of Jo didn't do her justice. She always looked pretty, but being in front of her now, she was a stunner. Her long, blonde hair fell around her in waves, and they didn't look to be placed there by some kind of hair equipment. She nibbled on her full lip as she appeared embarrassed by her friend's blatant pimping. Her blue eyes held a hint of promise, and her body, damn! He wanted to fuck her so badly. Just watching her, he was hard.

Big, juicy tits and rounded hips. Not to mention thighs that were designed to be wrapped around his waist as he fucked her.

He wanted her, no doubt about it.

Mandy had been dropping hints for a couple of months, constantly talking about the best friend with the cheating ex.

He couldn't believe anyone would cheat on this woman, unless she had some freaky tendencies.

"Well, Mandy does speak highly of you. It makes a change for her to, you know, talk about a guy without swearing."

Doc chuckled. "She's been asking me to date you for a while."

"Oh no, she hasn't, has she?"

"I believe she has commented that your dick of a

husband doesn't know what he's doing in the sack." Jo covered her face with a moan. "Told me that I look like the kind of guy you need."

"You're kidding me, right? Please tell me you're joking."

"No joke," he said. "Let me buy you a drink." He knocked on the counter. "Slick, now!"

"I'm so sorry, sir," he said.

Slick was twenty-three years old and wanted to be one of the Nowhere Men. He had zero muscle, but his loyalty was there. They just needed to be able to rely on him, and that would come with time and training.

Within seconds, they had a drink.

"Oh, Mandy." Jo looked out toward the dance floor. "Figures. She can make anyone dance with her."

"She's with my son," he said. Dale was one of the club brothers, and a man he'd trust with his own life.

"Wow, you have a son?"

"Yes."

"He … erm … you must have been young." She shook her head. "I'm so sorry. I'm really not used to this."

"You've just split from your husband."

"Officially divorced, actually."

"First husband? Second?" he asked.

"First and only. I don't think I'll be going that route again. You?"

"Never married. Never will. I was fifteen when I had Dale."

"Fifteen? His mother?"

"She was twenty."

"How did that—erm? Isn't that illegal?" Jo asked.

"You look cute when you're uncomfortable."

She paused, closing her eyes. "I'm sorry. I don't know exactly what I'm supposed to be."

"Nothing. His mother didn't want him, and seeing as my dad didn't want Dale adopted or put into foster care, I took him. He's my son, and the moment I held him, I knew I'd do anything for him." At fifteen years old, it hadn't been easy. He did learn to bag his dick up, and he'd never had another kid . Never found a woman he wanted. Dale's mother was a rich chick who wanted to have a bit of rough before she went back to her life. From what he knew, she was now married to some billionaire with a couple of kids. Dale wanted nothing to do with her, and she didn't want anything to do with him.

It was a win-win for him in all regards.

"Do you have any kids?"

"No, none. Mitch didn't want any children." She laughed. "I sound like a dumb trophy wife. I'm sorry. Mandy wanted to set us up. This isn't going great."

"Why not?"

It wasn't a normal date or even a hook-up conversation, but he rather liked to watch Jo. She didn't hide. Her emotions were plain to see.

He liked that.

"You're finding this comfortable?"

"We've gotten all the tricky stuff out of the way. You're divorced, no kids. You want to fuck someone that isn't your husband. Me, have a kid, I was young. No wife, no other kids, and I'd be happy to fuck you, sweetheart."

"You're as blunt as Mandy."

"She's got a lot of catching up to do. Life is too short, and I've got a lot of shit going on. I don't like to play around. You want to have some fun. I'm your guy. I'll be up front. I don't do love or marriage, or settle down. I fuck. I have fun. End of story. Don't go thinking this is anything but."

He took a sip of his beer, wondering if he'd been

too blunt, and then got confused by his own thoughts. Why should he give a fuck if he'd shocked her? He wasn't here to mess around.

Mandy had been dropping hints about Jo for weeks, and even though he didn't bite during any of them, it didn't mean he wasn't intrigued. He liked Mandy. She was a hard worker for him. She talked too much, but it was refreshing to have someone like her around. She put everyone at ease.

Jo took a long gulp of her beer, and he watched her throat work. All he wanted was to have those lips wrapped around his dick as he pumped his load deep into her throat, watching her swallow every single drop.

She licked her lips and stared at him. "I didn't ask for love. I may have been a useful wife, putting him through school, but it got old real fast. I'm happy to have some fun if you are."

Now he was getting somewhere.

Chapter Two

From standing in a biker bar, ordering a beer, to a conversation, to sitting in Doc's office, Jo didn't have a clue what the fuck actually happened. One minute she was embarrassed by Mandy's insinuations. Her best friend didn't have a subtle word or bone in her body.

Now she was sitting in Doc's office. The scent of leather, cigarette smoke, and beer was heavy in the air. She didn't detect any scent of sex, not that she'd have a clue. To know what the smell of fucking was like, she would have had to be having some.

There hadn't been a spark in her marriage in a long time. She hadn't slept with her ex-husband for some time before she caught him cheating. They didn't connect, and it was hard to want to have sex with a man who looked like it was a chore to be in the same room as you. After finding him in that compromising position, she got herself tested, and was clear.

Sipping at her beer, she had no idea where to look. This was all new to her.

"I'm curious, how many men have you fucked?" Doc asked.

Returning her attention to him, she pressed her lips together, feeling put on the spot.

"Erm, I don't think that's really any of your business."

"You look like a virgin, waiting to be taken and ravished."

Her cheeks had to be red. Her face was flaming hot.

"I'm not a virgin. I've had one partner."

"Your husband."

"Guys weren't exactly pushing down my door. What about you?"

"I've had too many to count."

"Really?"

He moved toward her, and even as she didn't want to, she took a step back.

"You don't even have an estimate?"

"A real man doesn't kiss and tell." He reached out, tilting her head back, and she stared into his eyes. He had the prettiest eyes, and from what she'd seen of his lips, she wanted them on her body, as well as his hands.

She wanted his kiss more than anything else.

"You're quite easy to read."

Jo didn't get a chance to respond as he slammed his lips down on hers, silencing any question or protest from her. With her hands clenched into fists at her sides, she didn't know what to do or to say.

Hold him.

Touch him.

Show him you're an actual human being with feelings and emotions.

She touched his arms, feeling the strength even through the leather of his jacket.

The hand that had rested beneath her chin moved, sinking into her hair. He grabbed the back of her head tightly, almost too much for her to handle. Her nipples went hard as pebbles.

Doc bit down on her lip, sucking it into his mouth before breaking from the kiss.

"This doesn't mean anything. You can fuck without regrets. No one is at home waiting for you. I won't judge you."

She closed her eyes, wanting it so badly. Her pussy was soaking wet, and she'd give anything to just let go.

Then do it.

No one is waiting for you at home.

You're lonely.

Stop being this woman that no one wants.

She was tired of curling up on the sofa each night, a tub of ice cream, and no one to share it with.

Sliding her hands beneath his jacket, she pushed it off his shoulders, breaking from the kiss to relish the sight as the jacket fell to the floor. She gripped his shirt, pulling it over his head and marveling at exactly how sexy he looked. His shoulders were thick and full of muscle, all covered in ink. Running her hands down his chest, she moaned as he pulled her close. He went to her shirt first, tugging it over her head.

She helped him get it off before dealing with her bra herself.

His groan mingled with hers as he cupped her tits. He pressed them together, leaning forward to slide his tongue across each peak.

"Fuck, you're beautiful."

To some women, having a bigger body was something to be embarrassed about. For Jo, she was happy in her skin. No matter her size or weight, she was happy with herself, and that was all that counted.

She had lost count of the number of times Mitch would tell her to go on a diet or to consider surgery. Each time she'd tell him to fuck off and leave her alone. She never let his cruelty get to her.

Pushing all thoughts of the ex out of her mind, she focused on the man who had promised her what she wanted.

His fingers slid down her body, and before she had a chance to, he was already popping open the button of her jeans.

She reached for his belt, tugging at it.

"For a little virgin, you sure know how to undress a man."

He finished with her jeans, shoving them down before she dragged his down and knelt in front of him.

Her face was on fire, but she wasn't going to back down. She wanted this, and what Doc offered, she really craved.

It was stupid, reckless, but it was something she wanted.

Without a second moment to doubt herself, she pulled down his boxer briefs, and his cock sprang out.

The cock was already swollen, pre-cum leaking out of the tip. Wrapping her fingers around the base of his cock, she took the head of his length into her mouth, moaning as his taste slid across her tongue. Closing her eyes, she took more of him until he hit the back of her throat, before pulling back.

She didn't release him as Doc gripped her head, denying her.

"Suck it properly."

Staring up the length of his body, she moaned around his dick as he went deep into her mouth. This time, she didn't stop. With her gaze still on him, she fought past her gag reflex and sucked him to her throat. Even as it was a struggle to breathe, she saw she'd taken him by surprise.

Jo may have had only one lover in her entire life, but that didn't for a second mean she came close to a virgin. She had skills that would blow Doc's mind, and she was no longer afraid to use them.

****

Rocking his hips, Doc filled her mouth, stretching those lips wide as she sucked him in deep. She took him, and as he pulled out, her nostrils flared as she took a breath. This woman knew how to deep-throat, and not only that, he was fucking addicted to the way her eyes were on him.

He had to listen to Mandy talk about this woman constantly. She truly believed he'd like her, and well, Jo on her knees, sucking his dick, what wasn't to like?

Knowing she'd only been with one man was a turn-on to him. He wanted to be the one and only man for her.

He yanked on her hair, pulling her mouth away from his dick. The length was covered in his pre-cum and her saliva.

He picked her up with ease. She wasn't a light woman, but her curves, he wanted them wrapped around him as he fucked her hard. Throwing everything off his desk, he placed her down on the center, spreading her thick thighs.

She was already so wet, and as he pressed his hand to her panties, he felt the dampness against his palm.

Sliding his fingers beneath the material, he pulled, tearing at the white fabric. For the rest of the night, she wouldn't be needing them.

Her pussy was nicely trimmed, and she looked so incredibly neat. Caressing through the smattering of curls, he heard her groan.

"Did sucking my cock turn you on?"

"Yes."

Her lips opened, and he stroked over her clit, loving the sound of her gasp and moan. He wanted to know exactly how tight she was, and as he slid his fingers inside her, this time, he groaned.

She was exactly how he imagined. Her pussy squeezed his fingers, and as he twisted inside, stroking her, she screamed his name.

He normally didn't like to hear a woman make her fake moans. With Jo, this wasn't fake. She wasn't trying to please him.

She was here because she wanted to be. Not for his President's patch. For his dick.

Doc couldn't help but smile.

Jo was using him.

It was a rather surreal feeling, but he'd been using a lot of women.

"How long has it been since a dick was inside here?" he asked.

"A year, maybe more. My husband and I hadn't been together for some time before I caught him cheating. I'm clean as well. I got tested."

"I'm clean." He was tired of talking. He held her pussy lips open and slid his tongue across her slit, sucking and nibbling at her. She was so fucking perfect and sweet. He stroked his tongue back and forth, around, and down to plunge inside her.

Jo rocked her hips up against his mouth. Her juices rubbed on his face as he couldn't get enough of her sweetness.

This was what he wanted more than anything. He also wanted to hear her scream her pleasure.

"Oh, fuck, that feels so good. Please don't stop."

As if he'd want to stop.

He sucked her entire nub into his mouth, using his teeth to bite down, and feel that explosion of pleasure as she came apart.

It didn't take long, and as he continued to please her with his fingers, he looked at her. "Was that fake?"

Her face was red, but the moment he'd been blunt with her, she'd been that way.

"No."

"Long time?"

"Very, very long."

He chuckled. Leaning over her, he reached into his desk drawer where he kept the condoms.

"I take it you're not protected against pregnancy?" he asked.

"No, I'm not."

He tore into the foil packet, sliding the latex over his length and rolling it to the base of his dick.

Once he was completely covered, he placed the tip of his dick at her entrance. She was already wet, so he wouldn't have any trouble filling her.

He wasn't small, and he hoped Jo could handle it.

Tonight, he didn't want to go slow or soft to get her accustomed to the feel of him. He wanted to fuck hard and to make her feel every inch of him.

Once the tip of his dick was inside her, he gripped her hips and slammed the rest of the way.

She cried out as he fucked her to the hilt.

He didn't give her the chance to get used to his dick as he pulled out and thrust in again hard.

"You okay?" he asked, taking her long and deep again.

She nodded, moaning. Her legs curled around his waist as he drove inside her, fucking her harder, making her cry out, filling her with his dick.

Her pussy was so tight, and as he stared down, she looked so pretty and red. Her opening pulsed around his length, and he wanted to come, needed to.

Reaching up, he cupped her hips, using them as leverage as he slammed into her, fucking her harder.

He'd long had his desk nailed to the floor, and now he was so glad as he didn't want to stop. He just wanted to keep on pounding inside her.

Lifting her legs up, he placed them over his shoulders and watched his cock as it sank deep into her.

The condom was covered in her cum, and he saw her cream as it smattered against her curls.

Seeing her arousal set him off, and as he fucked

her harder, he couldn't bring himself to stop. She was incredible, the feel of her pussy so good.

She wanted this, and knowing that was even more of a turn-on. Jo was here for herself, and he was going to take pleasure in that. His balls tightened, and he felt ready to explode.

The moment he did, he stared into Jo's eyes as he filled the condom.

In the back of his mind, he couldn't help but wonder if one day, he'd be filling her cunt with his cum instead.

Chapter Three

One week later

"Why haven't you seen him again?" Mandy asked.

Pouring them both a large glass of wine, Jo glanced over at her best friend. "You're asking me about your boss and the fact I slept with him?"

"Yes, and even though I saw you sneak out, you had this big smile on your face. You can't tell me it wasn't hot." Mandy giggled.

"You really want to know?"

"Of course I want to know. Doc's been asking about you."

Jo accidentally spilled some of the wine over the glass. "He has?"

"Yes."

She didn't know what to do about that.

"He likes you."

"Stop, Mandy. Seriously. It was one time."

"It was one great time."

"Why don't we talk about you and his son?"

Mandy wrinkled her nose. "There's nothing to talk about."

"Just like there's nothing to talk about with me, and yet you're determined to get me to talk about something. It was a one-time thing."

Her doorbell rang.

"Are you sure about that?"

"He doesn't know where I live. It's probably the pizza guy delivering to the wrong house again."

Mandy muttered something else, but Jo didn't exactly catch it. She headed to the front door, and without even looking through the peephole, she opened the door. It wasn't like anything bad ever happened in the town.

Doc stood at her front porch.

"Oh," she said.

"I didn't mean to disappoint you."

"You don't disappoint. She thought you were the pizza delivery guy."

"You get those kinds of calls a lot?" he asked.

"A couple of times." She brushed some hair out of her eyes. "What are you doing here?"

"It's a clear night. Beautiful. I figured we could take a ride."

"Yes, she would love to take a ride. Any kind of ride with you," Mandy said.

Jo looked behind her at her friend.

"I'll house sit. I've got nothing to do."

"Dale's looking for you."

"Exactly."

"You're giving my boy the runaround?" Doc asked.

"I'm just making sure he knows it was just a little fun. You understand, don't you?"

Doc glared at Mandy but didn't say anything else to her. To Jo, he asked, "What do you say?"

"She says yes."

"I need to hear it from her lips."

"Jo's shy."

"Jo's right here, and she doesn't need you guys talking about me as if I'm not here. So, a ride. A casual ride."

"On my bike."

"You know you always wanted to do that."

She wanted to kill Mandy.

"Sure, why not?" She glanced down at her clothes and groaned.

"You look fine."

She was in a pair of sweatpants and a really old shirt that hung off her. It was several sizes too big but one of the comfy shirts she loved to wear to rest and relax.

"Okay."

Grabbing her jacket off the coat stand, she sent Mandy a glare to let her friend know she was pissed at her.

Following behind Doc, she came to a stop at his very dominating bike. It was big, black, and it looked scary.

"It won't bite," he said.

"So it's the rider I've got be careful of."

"I'll bite you and make sure you like it."

She smiled.

Doc climbed on, and she nibbled her lip.

"What is it?"

"Don't I have to wear a helmet?" she asked. She'd never ridden a bike in her life. This was all entirely new territory for her.

"Nope. We'll take it slow."

She didn't see a reason to hesitate and climbed onto the back of his bike. He took hold of her hands, showing her how to hold onto him. He was strong, and as the engine roared to life, she let out a little gasp.

This had to be the most exciting and terrifying thing she'd ever done in her whole life. He took them on a road that went straight past his garage, the MC clubhouse, and out of town. The moment they passed the border sign, she couldn't help but relax. She'd made it this far. Leaning back a little, she closed her eyes and basked in the feel of the wind rushing through her hair and the happiness as Doc controlled the roads.

After nearly an hour, he pulled into a gas station to fill up the bike. The station was a late night one, and she climbed off the bike, feeling her legs quiver. She didn't need any help standing, and she turned to Doc, feeling invigorated.

"I had no idea it could be like that."

"Riding is the joy of life."

"Is that why you do it?"

"Among other reasons. The jacket is a chick magnet."

She laughed. "So I'm lucky to have your attention now."

"I figured you and I made an agreement."

"An agreement?"

"I'll scratch your itch and you'll do the same with mine."

"Sex?"

"You got it, baby."

"I thought we agreed to the one time."

"Is that what you think?" He stepped up toward her, stroking her cheek.

"You should be filling up with gas."

He pressed his cheek against hers. "I should be filling that tight pussy with my dick. Tell me you've not been wanting the exact same thing. I'll walk away now, not look back if you tell me the truth."

She pulled back to look him in the eye. She didn't speak a word.

It had been a week since their time together in his office. She had thought about him constantly, even when she tried to ignore all thoughts of him.

It shouldn't be this hard, and yet, it had been exactly that.

Doc had ruined her for everyone else, and even though she wanted to be strong, she couldn't be. She wanted him, and being single, why couldn't she have him?

Nothing was stopping her.

He winked before turning away.

This wasn't love. This was sex. Hard fucking, nothing more.

****

Doc never, ever brought a woman back to his home. It was strictly off-limits. He didn't even allow the club pussy to clean his space. He hired professional cleaners for this place. Yet, he invited Jo right inside.

His cock could be sucked and fucked by anyone. He didn't know what was so special about this woman. He had been with plenty of women, too many to count, and yet here he was, panting after this one.

Jo glanced around the main sitting room. "You have a nice place."

"You do know Dale's at your place screwing Mandy right now."

"So long as they don't do it in my bed or on my kitchen counters, I don't care. I've got a thing about my bed."

He laughed. She spun around until she finally faced him.

"You and I both know you didn't bring me here for chit-chat."

She lifted her shirt over her head and wriggled out of her sweatpants. She was right; he hadn't.

Removing his jacket, he placed it on the back of the sofa, watching her body as she moved. Within a matter of seconds, she was naked and walking toward him. He loved that she didn't try to hide her body from him.

The sway of her hips was a draw to him. He loved holding her hips as he pounded inside her.

She got to him, moving him so that he was in front of the sofa and pushing him down. She tugged his pants down, throwing them across the room.

"I should make you fold them."

Jo straddled his waist, and he liked a woman who took control, who wasn't afraid to go after exactly what she wanted.

"I could go and fold them, or I can fuck you, Doc. Which is it going to be?" She took possession of his lips, and he sank his fingers into her hair, holding her tight as he kissed her back.

She bit down on his lip, and his cock hardened.

"Please tell me you've got a condom," she said.

"In my wallet that's in my pants."

She groaned but climbed off him.

He ran his hand up and down his length watching her as she bent over, pulling out his wallet. He had nearly a grand in cash in there, but all she was interested in was the condom.

Jo put the wallet down and moved toward him. She had the latex on his dick in seconds and was back to straddling his waist. She pushed his hand out of the way, holding his cock and sinking down, inch by inch, onto his hard length.

He took hold of her hips and slammed her all the way down on his cock. "If you're going to fuck me, sweetheart, do it properly." He pulled her off his cock, only to pull her back down.

She gasped, her head falling back as he filled her, going as deep as he could. She gripped his shoulders and used him as leverage so she could ride his dick.

He stared down at where they were connected. The only way this could have been better was to feel her naked cunt wrapped around his length. One day soon, he wasn't going to be wearing a condom.

After Dale was born, he had sworn off all kids, but the idea of Jo being pregnant, of him having a reason to own this woman, shook him to the core. He wanted that. To have a reason to own her, to claim her for himself.

Was it selfish of him?

Yes.

Did he give a fuck?

No.

He shoved her to the sofa, lifting her thighs and using them as leverage to pound her pussy.

"Touch your clit. Get off, Jo. Let me feel you come all over my cock."

She strummed her clit, and he groaned, feeling her pussy quiver around his dick. It felt amazing, and he knew he wasn't going to last.

He watched her get herself off, feeling that build within her just before she cried his name. The sounds echoed off the wall as he pounded inside her. He wasn't gentle or quiet as he came.

When he did, he tried to get to the hilt within her as he spilled his cum. The condom was a distraction as he imagined his sperm taking seed inside her.

He didn't know the first thing about this woman, and yet he wanted to get her pregnant.

He was a fucking idiot.

She chuckled. "Wow, I have no words."

"You like my dick, don't you?"

"I'm not going to complain."

He pulled out of her pussy. His cum was still in the condom, but he held her legs up, watching her wet cunt. Not only did he look at her there, but he also couldn't help but stare at her tiny asshole.

Holding both of her ankles in his, he rubbed his fingers through her natural arousal, drawing it back to that little puckered hole.

"What are you doing?"

"We can have whatever we want from each other, right?"

"Right?" She didn't sound so sure.

"Have you ever had anyone fuck your asshole?"

"No, of course not."

"Don't sound so disgusted. You'd be quite surprised just how good it feels to have a cock here."

"You've tried it? I'd like to see that."

He chuckled. "Stop worrying. I won't try it now, but one day soon, I'm going to claim this asshole for my own, and I'm going to show you just how good it can be." To make a point, he pressed against her anus. She was tight as he knew she would be, but he wasn't going to give up. Stroking her ass, he stared into her eyes and watched.

There was intrigue there. She was curious, and he could live with that. There were so many dirty things he wanted to do with Jo, and he wasn't going to let her hide from her kinky self. It was time for her to explore this side of herself.

Chapter Four

Not once in all the years of Jo's marriage to Mitch had she let him do that to her. There was no denying Doc. From the first stroke of her asshole, feelings ignited within her, and she just couldn't control herself. She spread her legs a little wider and tilted her ass up for more.

"You're a dirty little slut, aren't you? I bet your husband couldn't handle you. Not the way I can."

She should call him out on bad-mouthing her, but right now, she couldn't even find the words to tell him to shut up and just touch her. She was addicted to his hands on her body, in need of it. In fact, the way he spoke to her turned her on. She knew she wasn't one, but it didn't matter.

Nothing that happened between them mattered.

"Look at your pussy. There's no denying you're enjoying this, Jo. You want this."

She whimpered as his other hand moved to her pussy. He slid two fingers inside her as his thumb teased over her clit.

He also started to fuck her with one finger, then a second in her ass. She bit her lip to try to contain her moans.

"I want to hear you, Jo. Let me hear you."

She cried out. "Please, don't stop."

"I have no intention of stopping. Your greedy pussy wants my hands, and I bet you even want my dick."

Her body was no longer her own as he worked her pussy and ass. She stared down at what he was doing as the burn in her ass intensified. It shook her a little at how expert he was in using her body or at least caressing her to get what he wanted.

"You're good at this."

"So's your mouth when it's wrapped around my dick."

He pumped his fingers inside her, his thumb flicking back and forth across her clit. She had heard of a woman having multiple orgasms, but she'd only ever experienced the rare one with a man.

She arched up as her orgasm rushed over her, taking her by surprise. The few seconds of pleasure made her writhe—she needed it, begged for it.

Doc wasn't done. He slowed down his strokes but prolonged her pleasure, waiting for her to slowly come down from her peak.

She couldn't stop, didn't want to, and as her orgasm ebbed away and Doc let go of her, she glanced down at Doc to see his cock already hardened against his jeans. Opening his jeans, she released his dick.

She wrapped her fingers around the length as she shuffled down his body. She moved so his knees were on either side of her head, and she took his cock into her mouth.

"You can use me any way you want," she said, releasing his cock with a pop.

He growled, gripping the back of her neck, and she moaned as he hit her throat. He fucked her mouth, and she watched him.

Doc was still in control, and she wanted to make him lose it.

Cupping his ass, she gave the firm cheeks a squeeze before spreading them. Sliding a finger across his anus, she began to stroke him.

He lost control, his actions becoming rougher as he fucked her face, going as deep as he could get, and she took him.

There were a few times he went a little too deep

and she gagged, but she loved watching him lose control.

This man, this leader, she wanted to shock him, to make him yearn for her.

Why?

This is just a little bit of fun.

She pushed all of her reasonings to the back of her mind as she worked his cock, moaning around the length, and when he finally came, she swallowed him down. Every single drop of cum that exploded, she gulped down, not letting any leave her mouth.

He pulled out of her and perched on her chest.

"You're going to be the death of me," he said.

"Yeah, well, this is the most fun I've had in a long time." She needed to keep on reminding herself this was just fun. She looked toward his clock. "It's a little after midnight. I'm going to have to go home."

"You don't have to go home. Dale and Mandy won't be done yet, and I don't want to catch my son's naked ass and in truth, I don't want to see Mandy naked either."

She laughed. "Are you really sure they'd be doing it in my house?"

"The tensions between those two have been rising for a couple of months now. Yeah, they will be fucking like rabbits."

She wrinkled her nose. "Rabbits are cute."

"Still fuck a lot though." He climbed off her chest and offered his hand.

"Either way, I still need to get home. Do you mind if I call a cab?" she asked.

"How about we compromise here and you stay the night?"

"How is that a compromise? I don't want you to start thinking I'm going to fall for you." She enjoyed their time together, even if it had only been two times now. When she was with him, all of her worries evaporated.

He cupped her face, and he pressed a kiss to her head. "I want you to stay. You know, a lot of women would get a kick out of being the first woman to stay here."

"Really? You think I'm going to fall for that one?"

"It's not a line. I don't bring women back here. This is my space, and I don't share."

"Oh."

"Yeah, oh. You can go back home by all means, but you can lay in your lonely bed listening to Mandy and Dale fuck, and think about what I could be doing to you instead."

"You're the devil."

"Nah, I'm not. Come on, let's shower." He led her back to his bathroom, which of course was way too tempting to deny.

There was nothing wrong with having a little fun.

Not tonight. This was what single people did. Any doubts she had, she pushed them aside. She didn't need to think about them.

****

Doc sipped at his coffee as Dale entered the office. One glance at Mandy's empty desk and whatever smile was on his son's face vanished.

"It's her day off. I figured you'd know that."

"You know where she is?" Dale asked.

"Probably out helping Jo." Mandy was with Jo. They were packing up the last of Jo's home. Even though she had gotten the house during the divorce, Jo wanted it gone. It was on the market, and from what he saw the other day, she would have no problem selling it.

"Fuck. I wanted to take her out to lunch."

Doc raised his brow.

"It's not what you think," Dale said.

"You're trying to court a woman that saw you riding three of the club pussy, and you think you've still got a shot?"

"Mandy understands things."

"Mandy knows a great deal, and she accepts a lot. Doesn't mean she's going to want you to herself." He knew Mandy was blunt and didn't beat around the bush. She made her feelings clear. She had already asked him if it was okay for her to have some fun with his son, nothing meaningful or long-lasting.

Mandy, behind all that bluntness, was a nice woman. Cute and sweet and if she let Dale get close, she'd be broken-hearted. It was one of the reasons he put up with her. She talked constantly, spoke her mind, but was also loyal.

She had been telling him about Jo and her divorce for months. How Mitch wanted to keep Jo, and had even offered them both an open relationship. From what Mandy knew, Mitch liked to play the field. He didn't want to sleep with his wife, but he liked having her as a security blanket. She was suitable to take to social gatherings, as his bosses liked a family man, but he didn't find her attractive. She was someone he wanted to use to better himself, but he also wanted to have fun without any consequences. Mandy had told him all the nitty-gritty stuff, and he saw the love she had for Jo.

He could see why. Jo was a sweetheart. She didn't make waves, and with Mandy working for him, he'd already known a great deal about Jo from the thorough investigation he'd gotten. No one worked for the Nowhere Men MC without being checked out.

"I like Mandy."

"You've had a lot of club pussy."

"Dad, that's been over for a long time. Don't talk to me about club pussy. You haven't had any either."

"You like Mandy. She's your age."

"Dad, come on, stop riding my ass."

Doc laughed. "Nothing much is going on here. We may as well pick up the girls some lunch and head on over to Jo's place." He wanted to see her.

After falling asleep beside her the other night, he'd woken up to find her gone. He didn't like it and couldn't think of a single reason as to why he could go and talk to her. Something casual didn't mean knowing their every waking moment, or talking on the phone just before they went to sleep.

He didn't date.

Had never dated.

Dale's mother had been a one-night stand, and to a fifteen-year-old kid, it had been an amazing night with a posh woman. Come the harsh reality of what it was, he'd regretted bedding her. Not for Dale though.

He loved his son more than anything in the world.

Having Dale around him day in day out was something he cherished.

After Doc climbed on his bike, Dale followed him into town, where they picked up some lunch before heading to Jo's house.

The front door was closed, but he saw Mandy's car parked in the driveway.

He parked his bike behind Mandy's car as Dale pulled in.

Grabbing their food, he didn't bother knocking, just walked right in.

Mandy was coming downstairs as he entered. "It's rude to not knock."

"I tell you that every single day, but you still barge into my office."

"That's work. This is a home."

"What is it, Mand?" Jo came out of the direction of the kitchen. Her long, blonde hair was pinned up on top of her head, and she wore a really nice pair of jeans that molded to her ass.

"We have invaders," Mandy said.

"What are you doing here?"

"Mandy told me what was going on, and I bought lunch. I figured we could help." Doc looked at his son, but he already had stars in his eyes, looking at Mandy.

When she was at the office, she always wore a dress, makeup, and let her hair full back. She looked out of place in the office, and she said it was to put female clients at ease. If they saw her looking like that, happy, it made them comfortable to be in the same room as the biker men.

It made a weird kind of sense, and he wasn't one to judge.

Today, she didn't look like a sweet woman. She wore jeans that were torn at the knees, a shirt that molded to every curve, and his son looked like he was panting for more.

Doc only had his eyes on one woman, and she looked nervous.

"I'll grab a few plates."

Leaving his son to his problem, he followed Jo.

"You abandoned me," he said, putting their bags of food down.

Jo stopped and turned to him. "I've never been the kind of person to do the day after."

"Not even with your husband?"

"Not even with him. It was all official by the time we slept together."

"He got a wedding ring on your finger?" he

asked.

"Pretty much. I don't want to keep talking about my marriage. It's over."

"You don't love him anymore?"

"No, I don't. I haven't loved him in a long time. The divorce was a relief." She put the plates on the counter.

Good to know.

He didn't want to start chasing after a woman if she was pining for her previous husband.

"You know, I didn't even cry when I caught him."

"You didn't?"

"Nope. It all made a lot of sense. I think I was more just happy to have a reason to divorce him."

Chapter Five

By the end of the day and with Doc and Dale's help, Jo was able to pack up the whole of her house. She had an apartment lined up for the end of the week, and Mandy had already agreed to help her move in.

Mandy and Dale made an excuse to leave before pizza even arrived, which meant she was alone with Doc. They sat on her sofa, eating their way through the pizza, and all the time she was aware of how close he sat. His thigh was brushing against hers.

He'd asked no end of questions as they packed, and she didn't have a clue why. She wasn't in love with her ex-husband anymore. Their time had passed, and she wanted nothing to do with him. Licking the cheese off her lips, she heard Doc moan.

When she turned to look at him, his gaze was on her mouth. "Do you have any idea what you do to me?" he asked.

"I've got some idea." She glanced down at the hard dick pressed against his zipper. It would be hard to miss what she did to him. She couldn't help licking her lips, and he took the pizza from her, smashing his lips down with hers.

"You know, I haven't fucked you on a bed yet."

"Mine is still made." She released a squeal as he lifted her up and started to carry her to her bedroom. He'd asked for a tour earlier, and seeing as they were helping her pack, she didn't see a problem.

He dropped her down to the bed, and before she knew what was happening, her tight jeans were off in one sweeping motion. Doc spread her legs, and as his hand touched her pussy, she groaned.

The pleasure was instant, intense, and she arched her pelvis up for him to give her more. So much more.

He stroked his fingers through her curls, teasing her clit before sliding down to push inside her.

She closed her eyes, took several deep breaths, and tried to focus as he flipped her over. He spread the cheeks of her ass wide, and she cried out as he teased across her anus.

Jo didn't have time to question him as he thrust in hard, taking her completely by surprise as he filled her. He pulled out, only to push in deep. All the time, his fingers teased across her asshole. She couldn't help but push back as he pulled out until only the tip was inside her.

"Stay still," he said.

His voice was deep, hard, and it made her ache to hear more. She didn't want him to stop talking to her. She felt hypnotized by the sound of his voice. There was nowhere else to go, not that she wanted to. She wanted all the kinds of dirty pleasure he could offer and for him to not stop.

Suddenly, he pulled out, and she whimpered. His fingers replaced his cock, sliding inside her wet pussy, teasing across her clit. When his teeth sank into her ass cheek, she cried out. The pleasure and pain were like a new drug that she couldn't say no to.

Doc worked her body like he knew the special tune to her instrument. He didn't stop until she came close to the crest, ready to spiral over, and then, he stopped.

"Please," she said, begging. She wasn't above begging. She'd been so close to coming, and now that he'd stopped, she wanted his touch again.

He chuckled. Doc was the one in charge, not her. She was his puppet, and he was the one pulling the strings.

Her teeth sank into her lip, and as his cock

pressed against her asshole, she was in no doubt as to what he wanted to do.

It was on the tip of her tongue to beg him to stop, but then, she couldn't bring herself to do it. She wanted this more than anything. Craved it.

Doc was giving her everything in life she'd fantasized about, and as he pressed the tip of that large dick to her anus, she didn't fight him, or argue.

She embraced the pleasure as he pushed past that tight ring of muscles, sinking inside her, going deeper than before, and she gritted her teeth, trying to calm her racing heart and failing.

"That's it, baby. I'm nearly all in." He reached between her thighs and stroked her clit, bringing her back to that peak as he sank the last few inches until he was as deep inside her as he could go.

This was pain but also pleasure. It was so much of each one that she didn't know which was stronger. As he stroked her clit, she didn't care as long as he made her come. That was all she wanted, and as he stroked her, he began to rock.

The feeling was too much and not enough at the same time.

After a few minutes or maybe even a couple of hours—she didn't know, time wasn't a factor—she began to press back, to fuck him hard, to want it.

When he finally pushed her into an orgasm, she screamed his name. The sound echoed around the room as he gripped her hips and took over. He didn't pound her. His strokes were long, deep, and shattering.

"Your ass is so fucking tight. You better get used to this, baby. I'm going to want you again and again."

He pumped into her ass, and she couldn't complain. Her orgasm was still sending aftershocks throughout her entire body.

When Doc came, she felt every single pulse as he filled her ass with his cum. His groan calmed her as he slowly pulled out.

She tried to move, but he held her still.

"What are you doing?" she asked.

"There's no better sight than seeing your cum leak out of your woman's ass."

What had she gotten herself into?

****

There were only a few things Doc was good at: leading the Nowhere Men, fucking, riding, and working on cars. He pulled out from under the hood of the latest piece of junk he'd been asked to fix.

The only other place in town was a complete butcher. They took cars and completely trashed them before they decided to come to him, to fix their babies. This latest one, he didn't know if he'd be able to fix it.

He had one other problem than the piece of junk. It came in the form of a beautiful, blonde, curvy woman, who'd come on his dick the other night and who he couldn't get out of his head.

"Here's the file you asked for," Mandy said, popping gum. "It's all the work the other place did before they decided to cut their losses."

She jumped up onto his workstation, waiting for him to glance through it. Dale had stopped by earlier, trying to convince Mandy to take the day off, but his secretary had refused. She had work to do. As her boss, he'd been more than willing to let her go out with his son, but he'd not intervened.

"How's Jo?" he asked.

"Can't get her out of your head, can you?"

He looked up from his paperwork. "I asked you a question."

"She's fine." Mandy pursed her lips.

"What are you doing with my son?"

"Nothing. I'm working. We both know what your son wanted, and last time I checked, I didn't read 'Dale's personal whore.'"

"You're playing with him?"

"Nope. Having fun is not playing. We're both consenting adults, but if you're going to have a hard time with that, I can stop it. I don't want to quit."

"I don't want you to hurt my son."

"That is not my intention. Believe me. Dale told me straight up he doesn't want to settle down, and he's not looking for love. Neither am I. I won't hurt your son, I promise. I'm following his rules, Doc. I bet you don't give a shit about the other women he's fucked and discarded. Remember that. I'm not blind to the workings of your club. I happen to like working here, but if it's going to be a problem, I can work anywhere."

"You think you can?"

"I've been in this town my whole life. Believe me, I'm adorable. I happen to like this job." She shrugged. "Jo moved into her new apartment. The house went through faster than she thought, and she's finally free of her dickface ex."

"She wasn't free before?"

"No matter how many spare keys she took from him, he always seemed to get inside the house."

"They're divorced."

"It doesn't mean it didn't hurt him in some way. Sure, he was cheating, but some lawyers like to have a certain image. Jo created that idea of Mitch being a family man. The kind of guy you could rely on. But look at you—thinking about her at work when you should be focusing on the car."

He closed the file, handing it to her. "The last couple of worksheets, I want you to reorder all the parts again. They paid for work that wasn't done properly."

He went to walk away, but Mandy slapped a piece of paper against his chest.

"Just in case you want to see her." She jumped off the counter.

"She said anything about me?" he asked, hating himself the minute the words left his mouth. He didn't give a fuck what anyone thought or felt.

Mandy chuckled. "She asked how you've been. If there have been any women sniffing around you. She's interested, Doc. Question is, what are you going to do about it?"

"I'm taking a break."

He threw down his cloth, heading to his bike. Glancing down at the address, he took off without a moment to question the reason as to why he was doing this.

Parking his bike, he made his way over to the apartment block. After locating her floor and her room, he knocked.

"Just a minute."

He heard her move around, and then finally, the door opened.

The moment she saw him, surprise flashed across her face.

"Doc."

"Mandy told me you moved."

"Yeah, it was a quick, spur-of-the-moment thing. You want to come in?"

She opened the door, and he stepped over the threshold. Her face was flushed. Her blonde tresses were pinned up above her head, and it had only been a couple of days.

He grabbed her around the waist and pressed her against the door, lifting her arms up.

"What are you doing?"

Doc slammed his lips down on hers, silencing any protest as he kissed her. Biting down on her lip, he heard the whimper but didn't care.

Breaking the kiss, he stared into her blue eyes.

"I missed you."

"This was supposed to be casual."

"It still is. Doesn't mean I don't want what I want."

"And what is it exactly that you want?" she asked.

He kept her hands pinned above her head as he slid his palm down to cup her large tit.

"I want to have a bit of fun."

"I thought that was what we were having, Doc. Some fun."

He stared at her. "You can't fuck anyone else."

"You're staking your claim?"

"Yes. No one else and the fun continues."

"What about you?" she asked.

"Me?"

"Yeah. You think I'm just going to take orders from you and not expect you to be exactly the same? Your other women may work like that, but me, I don't. I want the same from you."

He sighed. "Consider it done. You better be enough for me."

She pulled her hand from where he held her still, cupping his dick. "And you better be enough for me, Doc."

"Works both ways?"

"You got it."

He laughed, and picking her up, he carried her across the apartment. The only reason he knew where the bed was that he saw it as her doors were all open. Her apartment was trashed, but he'd help her sort through that once he had his fill of her.

Chapter Six

Jo's second biker party was very different from her first experience. This one, there were a lot more bikers, and Doc didn't let her out of his sight. Drinks were brought to her by other members or some of the women. She never drank any from the women of the club. They'd been giving her the evil eye ever since Doc had brought her around to the club and officially declared her as his.

She didn't entirely know what that meant, but the men gave her wide berth. She didn't think it meant she had some kind of rotten disease, but the way the men acted, she couldn't help but wonder if that wasn't the case.

Still, the nights were spent with them using each other, and she rather liked seeing Doc lose control. The moment they were alone, all bets were off, and they were incredible together.

She hummed to herself as she glanced around the clubhouse's back yard. She tapped her foot to the tune of the music and smiled when she saw Mandy finally arrive.

Her best friend approached, looking sexy as hell.

"Look at you." Jo made to pull away, but Doc gripped her arm. "I just want to say hi."

Mandy laughed. "Don't worry, Doc, I'll keep her safe."

Jo rolled her eyes.

Doc pulled her in close, and right there, for all to see, he kissed her hard.

"Possessive much?" Mandy asked, placing her arm through hers and escorting her away from the boring, macho conversation going on around her. She wanted nothing to do with any of it.

"I've been waiting for you, forever."

Mandy chuckled. "I know. I had to get changed."

"What is going on with you and Dale?" Jo asked, spotting the man himself watching her.

"Not a whole lot. We have some fun, but that's about it." Mandy shrugged her shoulder. "Let's go and get a drink."

They headed over to the bar where a couple of the women were. The moment they saw her, they all turned their backs.

"What's the matter, you don't like how she's taken your Prez?" Mandy pouted as she grabbed them both a drink.

They found a small bench near the fire. Taking a sip of the beer, Jo sighed. "I don't think I'll ever get used to them hating me."

"With all due respect, what does it matter? Most of them fuck all the club members, Jo. I wouldn't worry about them. They'd likely push you out of the way to be the one claiming the old lady tag from Doc."

"Is the old lady tag as bad as it sounds?"

Mandy laughed. "No. It just means you're not club property. No guy has a right to have his way with you."

"You don't have to romanticize it."

"Guess who dropped by my place before I left?" Mandy asked.

Jo shrugged. "Not a clue."

"Mitch. He said he was looking for you."

Jo groaned. "What did you say?"

"What? I'm a nice girl."

"You always have a way of pissing him off."

"Last time I checked, you didn't wear his ring. What does it matter? He needs to learn that he lost you. His wayward dick lost him the best woman he's ever going to have."

"I love you, you know that?" she asked.

"I know."

"What did you say?"

"I called him a dickless wonder. What? It could have been worse."

"But you didn't have to actually say anything to him," Jo said.

Mandy took her hands. "Listen to me, honey, you don't have to think about him, worry about him. The entire point of divorce is he stops being our problem. Stop making him yours."

Jo took a breath. "You're right." She looked toward Doc, and her whole body went on alert when she found him looking right at her. The heat in his eyes was hard to ignore. Biting her lip, she turned back to Mandy, smiling.

"You like him?"

"I do."

"Then go and lure him away with those sexy eyes of yours. I'm going to go and have some fun." Mandy gave her hands a squeeze.

Jo sipped her beer, getting to her feet and moving away from the noise of the party. She knew Doc had followed her, felt him against her back as he moved close.

He pulled some of her hair off her shoulder, and his lips brushed across her neck, making her gasp.

"All I want to do is fuck you," he said. He growled the words against her neck, and she couldn't help but moan at the pleasure that rushed through her body.

"Please," she said.

"You want me to fuck you?" He gripped her hips, and she couldn't move as his hand slid between her thighs. "I believe you were put on this earth to drive me insane." He loosened the top button of her jeans. She was already soaking wet, and as his hand slid inside her panties, he felt it as well. His growl confirmed it.

He took her behind one of the dirty sheds. He placed her hands on the hard wood, telling her not to let go. Within seconds, her jeans were around her ankles and he was inside her. His cock, long and hard, branded her as he fucked her.

Doc bit down on her neck, making her cry out, and she just couldn't fight it, didn't want to. This was so wrong to be out in the open where anyone could find them, but when it came to Doc, all common sense left her.

There was no logical thought, just feelings, intense, all-consuming need as he pounded inside her, branding her as his.

She'd never been like this with any man, and part of her feared she'd never be the same. Doc was taking more than her body; he was taking a part of herself, and she knew there was no coming back from this.

****

Several weeks later, Doc picked Jo up and carried her across the parking lot.

"Let me down!" She was giggling, and instead of beating his ass, she was squeezing the cheeks.

In the past couple of weeks, she'd pretty much moved into the clubhouse, and he didn't have a single problem with that. Dropping her down onto the back of his bike, he cupped her face and slammed his lips down on hers. The moan he heard was enough to make his dick incredibly hard. He loved having her around the clubhouse. She was in easy reach, and he liked looking at her. Not only that, she was also amazing to talk to. She asked him never-ending questions about his life. Nothing to do with the club or club business but about *him*.

Where he grew up. Why he became a mechanic. The reasons he loved action movies. What was his greatest achievement in life.

All the real-life questions couples talk about with each other.

The one question he hadn't asked Jo yet was about kids. He'd noticed her interest in them, and whenever they passed a family while they were out enjoying their time together, he saw the longing in her eyes.

Part of him was afraid to broach the subject. He didn't know what her ex was like or if she could even have kids.

Dale was his only son, and he'd not given it a lot of thought about having another.

Holy shit!

He was thinking about it.

Breaking from the kiss, he saw her sweet smile.

"That was incredible," she said.

"Yeah, there's a lot more where that came from."

The sound of a car coming to a harsh stop drew their attention. Doc didn't recognize the guy, but he sensed the change in Jo. She tensed beneath him.

"Do I want to know who this guy is?" he asked.

"He's my ex."

"Like ex-husband ex?"

"The one and only." She climbed off the bike and stepped in front of him. "What do you want, Mitch?"

"I have to listen to the rumors about you at the diner, and that's all you've got to say to me? Do you have any idea what your … relationship is doing for my reputation?"

Doc tensed up, and one glance behind him, he saw the club already making their way toward him.

The club adored Jo. It probably helped she had a

wicked sense of humor and she never tried to hide from him. She always stood toe to toe. Even though they'd only known each other a month, tops, he knew she was special.

"What does it matter?" she asked.

"Do you have any idea what it is you're doing?" he asked. "What you could be doing to me? You got the house, and a nice sum every single month. You completely ruined my reputation as a lawyer because you won, and now, you're screwing around with this trash! Do you have any idea what this could be doing to me?"

She burst out laughing. "Seriously? We're divorced. If anyone should be worried about reputations, it's me when it comes to yours. You couldn't even keep it in your pants long enough. You cheated on me. I've moved on. I'm happy."

"Leave," Doc said.

He wrapped his arm around Jo, holding her close, wanting to protect her.

"Are you fucking serious right now?" Mitch asked.

"You're not doing yourself any favors here, dick-face," Mandy said. "I told you that you never deserved her, and guess what, I was right. You don't. She's moved on, and unless you want all of your bullshit and lies spread across town, you should leave."

Doc watched as Mandy stepped right up to Mitch, clearly not afraid. Jo pulled out of his arms and did the same.

"Don't come around here anymore, Mitch. What I have going on with Doc is my business. If you want to start something, we can. You will always be in the wrong."

Mitch opened his mouth, closed it, and Doc watched as the fight left her ex. "Can we talk?"

"No," Jo said.

"Come on, Jo."

"I said no. The time for talking ended when you had sex with another woman. Some can forgive. I can't, and I won't. Besides, I don't love you anymore." She turned her back on him and walked up to Doc. She went to her toes and kissed him on the lips. "I'll see you later."

Doc nodded, watching her go with Mandy. The two women were walking hand in hand, out of the clubhouse.

"I didn't read this wrong, right?" Dale asked. "She's more than a quick fuck to you?"

"Dale, you're my son, but that doesn't mean I won't whip your ass."

His son burst out laughing. "I love it when you get all violent."

"I love her," he said.

"Holy shit! You do?"

"Yes."

"Wow, that is a giant leap from just sex," Dale said.

Doc turned toward Dale. "You got a problem with her?"

"No. I don't have any problem. As it happens, I'm in love with Mandy. You got any advice on how to tame that wildcat?" Dale asked.

Doc burst out laughing. "Get yourself a new wildcat."

"Not going to happen. Only one woman I want and I'm going to win her over, you'll see."

Leaving his son to figure out how to win over Mandy, Doc made his way into his office and pulled open the office drawer. He didn't know why he'd gone and picked out an engagement ring just last week. He was the one to set the boundaries between himself and

Jo. Sex. That was all it was supposed to be, but he didn't want her for just fucking.

Walking through town, even taking her riding, he saw guys appreciated her lush curves and sweet smile. She had a body to fuck and the face of an angel. A woman like her shouldn't be with a guy like him, and he didn't want to share. He didn't want to lose her. She was everything, and she'd become so in such a short time that it fucking scared him.

He wanted to stake his claim on her so no one else had a chance. He hadn't become the president of the Nowhere Men MC without knowing what he wanted.

This was one fight he was determined to win.

Chapter Seven

"No, no, no, no, no." Jo groaned, panicking with each passing second as she picked up each of the four pregnancy test kits she'd purchased. Each kit held two tests. She'd promised herself she wouldn't be one of these women who picked up a load of kits and didn't believe the first answer, yet here she was.

She was pregnant with Doc's child.

There hadn't been any other man, and they'd only had unprotected sex a couple of times. She knew it only took once, but this was just unfair.

Could she be excited about this?

It seemed next to impossible to be happy about this.

Doc didn't talk about kids. *She* didn't talk about kids. There was no talk of any kind when it came to kids, and yet she was pregnant. This seemed like the world's worst luck.

She placed a hand on her stomach, taking a deep breath. Doc wanted to meet up with her for lunch, but right now, she felt like the worst person in the world. She was so happy right now.

Her life was finally on track after the divorce, and she couldn't help but be scared this could ruin it. If Doc didn't want to be part of their baby's life, then she could handle it. Being a single mother was tough, but if that was what she had to do, she'd do it.

Getting to her feet, she threw all the tests into the trash. Staring at her reflection, she forced a smile to her lips. She looked a little pale and her hair slightly damp.

Before heading out for lunch, she took a quick shower to freshen up.

She opted for a skirt and shirt, a pair of pumps, and she pinned her hair back. Just as she finished with the last pin, the doorbell rang.

She'd given Doc the code to her apartment so he could let himself in whenever he wanted.

"Hello, beautiful," he said, the moment she opened the door. She didn't get a chance to respond as he cupped her hip and kissed her.

He'd only ever promised her a good time, and she needed to remember that.

Doc pulled away. "You okay?"

"Yeah, yeah, I'm fine. Can we go?" she asked.

"I need to take a leak first. Gunther was on the shitter, and it stunk."

"Colorful."

She watched him go to her bathroom without waiting for an invitation.

"Oh, shit, wait, you can't go." She rushed toward the bathroom, storming into the room in time to see Doc already taking a leak, but he was also holding the pregnancy test boxes in the other hand.

Neither of them spoke as he finished. She turned away, waiting for him to clean himself up.

The water ran, and she turned to see him washing his hands before wiping them on the towel. She did like his cleanliness.

"What is this?"

"You know what it is." Her cheeks were on fire, and she felt sick to her stomach. She took a deep breath, hoping she didn't throw up.

She was still hungry.

"Is it yours?" he asked.

"The baby?"

"No, the boxes. You took these?"

"Yes."

"Holy shit," he said.

She nibbled her lip, feeling tears spring to her

eyes. "I … I…"

"When do we have a doctor's appointment?" he asked.

"What?"

"We need to get you checked out. Make sure everything is fine. Fuck, I can't, I won't sleep with you. Sex is out of the question." He rushed toward her, his hand landing on her stomach. "Are you okay? How do you feel? I thought you looked pale the other day, but I didn't want to upset you."

"You noticed?"

"Of course I noticed. When it comes to you, I notice everything."

"Oh. You're not going to ask if this is your baby?"

"I know it's mine. I trust you, Jo."

"This was only supposed to be sex." She stared into his eyes, waiting for something, desperate to find anything to say this was something more.

She couldn't see any signs, and it scared her.

"It was sex, but now it's a whole lot more. You're going to marry me."

"Whoa, whoa, wait a minute. No one said anything here about marriage. I already got out of a bad one."

"You don't have a choice."

"You didn't marry the other mother." She frowned. "You know what I mean."

"There's a difference."

"There is? Enlighten me then."

"Simple, I didn't give a flying fuck about Dale's mother. She was a quick, easy fuck."

"And I'm not?"

"No." He gripped her ass, holding her against his side. "You're mine, Jo. The moment you entered that bar, you became mine. The moment I sank my dick inside your pussy, you were mine."

"I get it, I get it. I'm yours."

"Damn straight you are, and that means my ring on your finger. You're my old lady. The crew all like and respect you. That baby is going to have my name, and you're going to be my wife."

"And I've got no choice in the matter?"

"Tell me you don't love me as much as I love you."

This made her pause. "You love me."

"I don't wear my heart on my sleeve for anyone, Jo. I knew you were trouble the moment you entered my club. I just didn't know how much."

"This is crazy. I can't believe we're even considering this."

"Crazy or not, it's happening. Sooner rather than later." He stroked her stomach. "Were you going to tell me?"

"Of course. I didn't expect you to go rummaging around in my trash though. I had hoped to have some time."

"I'm a nosy bastard. Can't help myself." He kissed her head. "I'll prove it to you."

"What?"

"That I love you."

She cupped his cheek, stroking her thumb across it. "You don't have to prove anything to me."

****

Doc had never been good with words or romance. When it came to Jo, he'd expected it all to be sex. Meaningless sex, or at least that was what he'd hoped. They were only supposed to use each other, but standing before Jo, three weeks after finding out she was pregnant, he was overjoyed as the priest announced them as man and wife.

He pulled her into his arms, and as all of his boys watched, he claimed her lips hard. The Nowhere Men MC cheered, and he heard Mandy's whistle. She was the only bridesmaid and maid of honor. Jo hadn't wanted a big affair, and just marrying in front of the club had been ideal for him.

Some of the club pussy weren't happy with the way he'd been taken off the market, but knowing he was going to be a father and the feelings he had for Jo, he didn't give a shit.

No other woman would do.

The only one he wanted was Jo, and everyone else would fall into line. He had no problems pissing others off. In fact, he rather saw it as a sport.

"You're all mine now," he said, tilting her head back to smile at her.

"You think that scares me?"

"Doesn't it?"

"Not a chance. The time for being afraid was when I first met you." She wrapped her arms around his neck, and he cupped her ass. Once again, his boys let out whistles. Jo's face went a nice bright red as she buried her head against his chest.

"Oh, God, I can't believe this is happening."

"Believe it, baby." He kissed her lips, her neck, and held her close. He wasn't in a rush to leave. They were at the clubhouse for a reason. He wanted her all to himself. "How are you feeling?"

"A little tired, but I've been told that's normal. Carrying two babies is a challenge."

He stroked her stomach, kneeling down to touch her and kissing their babies. Her stomach wasn't showing any real signs of being pregnant but that wouldn't be long now.

He couldn't wait to see her heavily pregnant with his kids. In fact, it made his balls ache just thinking about it.

"Doc, everyone is watching?"

"They all know I've knocked you up, babe."

"Charming."

"That's me, charming all over." He stood up, holding her in his arms. "I really do love you, you know."

"You keep on saying that."

He stroked a curl back from her head, and was completely hypnotized by her smile. "I mean it."

She ran her hands over his chest. "I know you do. I love you too."

He'd never believed in love. For a long time, he'd been cynical about a lot of married couples as he truly believed they moved too fast. To finally find the woman meant for him and to have her all to himself, he couldn't imagine being with anyone different. She was everything, and he knew he was lucky to have her.

The priest bade them goodbye, and with Jo at his side, he watched the priest leave, before heading back to the party. He didn't let Jo go all night, dancing with her. Even when a couple of the guys tried to take her away to dance, he wouldn't let her go, not even with Mandy, who was trying to avoid Dale.

He didn't know what was going on between his employee and his son, but he made a note to keep an eye on them.

"So, you now have me all to yourself, Doc, what is it you're going to do with me?" she asked.

"Blow your mind with just how happy I'm going to make you."

Epilogue

Seven months later

Holding onto Jo's hands, Doc had no choice but to grit his teeth and endure the pain as his wife screamed. She pushed, and he kissed her head, holding her, hoping the little shits would come out of her soon.

If he ever had a single doubt of his feelings about this woman, he no longer did. He was fucking furious. She had kept the pain levels and the contractions to herself until he'd woken up to her whimpering.

He'd gone to the bathroom that night to find her with a damp towel between her teeth, sweat beading her forehead. She had finally told him she needed to go to the hospital.

There hadn't been enough time to get her signed in, but with how late it was, the doctors escorted her straight to labor. That had only been five minutes ago, and now, his son and daughter were being stubborn.

They were hurting her, and he couldn't stand to hear her pain.

Finally, after what felt like an eternity, a scream filled the air. The sound was strong and fierce. Doc didn't dare look, just in case something happened.

His men had taken the piss out of him for all the pregnancy books he'd read. He hadn't cared with Dale's mother. She had been nothing more than a quick fuck that had resulted in a pregnancy.

With Jo, he paid attention.

He was at every single doctor's appointment, and all of the classes she wanted him to go to. Regardless of how he made people feel, he was there for her.

"One more push, baby," he said. "One more push."

"I'm so tired."

"I know. I know. You're amazing. You're stunning. You're beautiful." He kissed her as the doctor tried to get her to push. "Come on, we're nearly done."

She sighed but grabbed his hands as she needed to push.

He held her, taking the pain as she squeezed down. Finally, another scream, and Jo collapsed against him, sobbing.

"They sound so beautiful," she said.

"They're ours, Jo. You and me did this."

The nurses came over, holding out two bundles.

One placed his little girl in his arms, as his son was given to Jo. He stood as close to her as he could.

"Are you okay?" he asked, worried for her.

"I'm … so happy. Look what we did," she said.

"You did this, honey. You brought these two angels into the world." He stared down at his daughter and at his son. "They're perfect. You've got a big brother. Both of you have a big brother. He's going to love you so much."

"Dale and Mandy, we've got to tell them."

"I will. I'll call them."

"What should we name them?" she asked.

"Rachel and Kyle," he said.

She chuckled. "You really like those names."

He stared down at the woman he loved. "As long as I have you, I don't care."

"I love those names." She turned to their babies. "Rachel and Kyle it is. You're going to be so loved."

Doc stayed with Jo until she fell asleep. With his two babies asleep in their crib, he left the room to let Mandy and Dale know about their birth. He hung up the phone and made his way back inside.

Moving onto the bed, he spooned his wife, wrapping his arms around her.

Kissing her neck, he closed his eyes, content, in love, and knowing that come morning, it was going to be hell.

He couldn't wait.

The End

SAM CRESCENT

EVERNIGHT PUBLISHING ®

www.evernightpublishing.com